TERROR
AT THE
ZOO

TERROR
AT THE
ZOO

Peg Kehret

COBBLEHILL BOOKS/DUTTON

New York

Library of Congress Cataloging-in-Publication Data
Kehret, Peg.
Terror at the zoo / Peg Kehret.
p.   cm.
Summary: Twelve-year-old Ellen and her younger brother Corey are
excited about their overnight camp-out at the zoo, until they discover
that they are locked inside with a desperate escaped convict.
ISBN 0-525-65083-0
[1. Zoos—Fiction.   2. Mystery and detective stories.]   I. Title.
PZ7.K2518Te 1992   [Fic]—dc20   91-25728   CIP   AC

Published in the United States by Cobblehill Books,
an affiliate of Dutton Children's Books,
a division of Penguin Books USA Inc.,
375 Hudson Street, New York, New York 10014
Designed by Joy Taylor
Printed in the United States of America
First Edition   10 9 8 7 6 5 4 3

Special thanks to Elaine Bowers, Carol Raitt, Katharyn Gerlich, Ira and Delaney Gerlich, Carrie Rhodes and Alex Alvord, and the Woodland Park Zoological Society, Seattle, WA.

*This book is dedicated, with love and gratitude,
to the women who gave birth to my children.*

TERROR
AT THE
ZOO

1

ELLEN STREATER looked across the yard at Prince, her German shepherd. Silently, she directed her thoughts to him: *Come, Prince. Come to me.* She didn't call his name aloud, or whistle, or clap her hands. She only sent her thoughts.

Prince quit sniffing the grass and turned to look at Ellen.

Come, Prince, she thought again. Then she closed her eyes and imagined Prince walking across the grass toward her.

When she opened her eyes, Prince stood in front of her, wagging his tail.

"Good dog," Ellen said. "What a fine dog." She patted Prince's head for a few moments and then wrote the date, time, her command, and Prince's response in her notebook.

Her experiment was turning out far better than she had expected. The last six times she had called him silently, Prince had responded. Once he even came when he was sitting under the big maple tree, waiting for a squirrel to come down. Prince had been trying all his life to catch a squirrel and was not easily distracted when he saw one. But when Ellen directed him, in her mind, to come, Prince took his eyes from the squirrel and walked straight to Ellen.

Ellen planned to enter her animal communication experiment in the annual All-City Science Fair. Her science teacher had suggested the subject last spring and loaned Ellen a book on animal communication.

Ellen had been skeptical of success, despite the claims in the book, but she had worked on her project all summer, carefully recording her efforts with Prince.

With summer nearly over, Prince frequently obeyed her nonverbal commands to come. Now she wondered if he might be able to understand other thoughts, as well.

She closed her eyes again, focusing all her attention on Prince. *Get your ball*, she thought. *Get your ball.*

"Hey, Ellen!"

Ellen's eyes flew open, startled by her younger brother's loud call.

Corey yelled again. "Mom says to tell you it's time to quit playing with Prince and get ready for dinner."

Ellen glared across the yard at him, her concentration shattered.

From the back porch, she heard her mother scold, "Corey! I could have shouted at Ellen myself. Next time, go out and speak to her quietly."

Prince loped toward the porch, hoping, no doubt, that he was going to get dinner, too. Ellen sighed and started

2

toward the house. She didn't know which irritated her more—Corey's yelling or the fact that her mother had instructed her to quit "playing" with Prince.

Mrs. Streater knew about Ellen's science fair experiment in animal communication. Why did her mother insist on calling it play, as if Ellen were still a little kid talking to her Barbie?

Today, of all days, Ellen thought, I should think Mom would realize that I'm finally mature.

Mature. She liked that word. As she washed her hands for dinner, she decided that this birthday was a turning point. Now that she was twelve years old, she would always act mature.

Maybe after tonight's birthday dinner, her parents would realize that Ellen was no longer their baby girl. Maybe they would treat her like a grown-up, for a change. Maybe they would quit lumping her together with Corey, as if she and her brother were Siamese twins, when he was a mere infant compared to Ellen.

The kids. That's how Ellen's parents always referred to her and Corey. "Let's take the kids to a movie." "Would you kids please clean up your rooms?" "Dinner's ready, kids."

Now that she was twelve (and Corey wouldn't be eight for two more weeks) surely her parents would realize she was no longer one of the kids. She was one of the adults.

"Hello! Where's our birthday girl?"

Ellen smiled as she heard her grandparents arrive. She was certain that Grandma and Grandpa would acknowledge her new mature status by giving her an appropriately adult birthday present. Grandma and Grandpa always seemed to know exactly what Ellen wanted, even when she didn't know herself.

Maybe they would give her a makeup kit or one of those big scarves that were so fashionable now. At least she could count on Grandma and Grandpa not to buy her a doll or some kiddie game, like the stupid one Corey wanted for his birthday.

Ellen hugged her grandparents. She noticed that they didn't carry a wrapped package. They put a large white envelope on the table where the other birthday presents were.

It's a gift certificate, Ellen thought. Maybe they bought me a make-over at a fashionable beauty salon. I'll get my hair styled and my nails manicured and I'll be able to pass for fourteen, if I want to.

The more she thought about it, the more she was positive that's what the envelope contained. She had been trying to grow her brown hair long enough to wear it in a French braid but meanwhile, it just flapped around her ears, like fringe on a blanket. A good styling salon would change that. She would be gorgeous. Well, maybe not gorgeous—even the best salons can't work miracles—but anything was bound to be better than her hair the way it was.

She decided to open the envelope last, to save Grandma and Grandpa's surprise for the very end. The grand finale.

After dinner and the birthday cake, and after she had opened a gift from her parents and one from Corey, she finally reached for the envelope from Grandma and Grandpa.

As she did, Grandma said, "Before you open that, we need to tell you that it is a joint birthday gift for you and Corey."

"You mean," Corey said, "what's in the envelope is half mine?"

"That's right."

Ellen could not believe her ears. A joint present with Corey? That infant? How could this be? If her present was something Corey would like, it would be way too babyish for her. Especially now that she was mature. And what about her hair? She tried to hide her disappointment.

"Do I get to see it today, too?" Corey asked. "Even though my birthday is still two weeks away?"

"Yes. We didn't want to make Ellen wait, so you get your gift early this year, Corey."

Ellen forced a smile as she opened the envelope. She didn't want to seem ungrateful, no matter how much she wished they had given her a present of her own instead of something to share with Corey.

There was a certificate inside the envelope. "What's it say?" Corey cried. "Hurry up and read it!"

THIS CERTIFICATE IS GOOD FOR AN
OVERNIGHT CAMP-OUT
AT THE WOODLAND PARK ZOO

Corey, who was leaning over her shoulder, read the words out loud and then let out a whoop.

"No kidding?" Ellen said. "We get to stay overnight at the zoo?"

Ellen loved the zoo. Grandma and Grandpa had given

her some good presents before but never anything like this. She forgot all about her hair.

"The zoo is closed at night," Corey said. "How will we get in? Are you sure they'll let us camp there? What if the zoo people call the police and have us arrested for trespassing on private property and what if we get taken to jail and locked up with the drug addicts and . . ."

"Whoa," Grandpa said, holding up his hand to silence Corey. Ellen knew Grandpa wasn't being rude. Sometimes you have to interrupt Corey when he gets started on one of his what-if stories. Otherwise he'd babble on all night.

"The camp-out was one of the auction items this year," Grandma explained.

Ellen knew which auction she meant. It was a charity auction, an annual event which benefited several community organizations. Grandma and Grandpa went to the auction every year and they always bought some unusual item donated by the zoological society.

Once they paid four hundred dollars for the chance to give an elephant a bath. With the elephant's trainer supervising, Ellen and Corey got to help Grandpa and Grandma wash Hugo, a gentle old African elephant. Another time, Grandma and Grandpa went fishing in the moat inside the lion exhibit. They were on the other side of the moat from the lions but still, it was pretty exciting.

Last year they bought a portrait with a python. Ellen thought that purchase was gross but Grandma and Grandpa had their picture taken with a humongous python draped around their shoulders, and sent prints to all their friends.

"We're going with you," Grandpa said. "The camp-out is for four people."

"When is it?" Ellen asked. "When do we go?"

"September tenth. Since your folks will be in San Francisco that week and we were going to stay with you anyway, we thought it would be the perfect time to do the camp-out."

"September tenth is Friday," Mrs. Streater said. "Dad and I will get in late that night. We'll come to the zoo in the morning to take pictures."

Corey scratched himself under both arms and made chattering sounds. "I want to sleep in the monkey house," he said.

Where he belongs, thought Ellen.

"The zoological society will decide where we sleep," Grandpa said. "Wherever it is, I'm sure we will have quite an adventure."

"Thanks, Grandpa and Grandma," Ellen said, as she gave them each a hug. Her smile was genuine now. Even though it wasn't a salon make-over, it certainly wasn't a babyish gift, either. Her parents still liked to go to the zoo. Lots of adults do. An overnight camp-out at the zoo would be wonderful, even if Corey was there, too. She went to the calendar and drew a big red circle around September tenth.

2

TONY HAYMES waited until a woman with two small children entered the secondhand store; then he went in, too. Kids would distract the clerk. Tony didn't know if the story of his escape from prison was on the news yet but the last thing he needed was for someone to recognize him.

He went straight to the housewares section and examined several trays of kitchen utensils before he spotted what he wanted: a sturdy butcher knife. Tony felt the six-inch blade with his thumb. Good. It was sharp and strong.

While the salesclerk helped the woman shopper find shoes that would fit her children, Tony slipped the knife up the sleeve of his jacket and left the store.

Too bad he'd lost the first knife, the one he stole from the prison kitchen, when he jumped. The rest of his plan had worked perfectly. He had crawled through the secret hole he'd cut in the roof of his cell, then slithered across the rafters in the attic and out onto the roof.

The jump from the roof to the top of the prison wall had been the big gamble. For weeks, Tony worried that he would miss, that he would fall and break a leg and be carried back inside the prison walls on a stretcher.

But September tenth was his lucky day. He had planned the escape for his birthday, thinking it would bring him good fortune and it did.

He didn't fall. All of the knee bends and push-ups in his cell, night after night, had resulted in a lean body with powerful muscles. When his hands hit the top of the wall he had swung easily over the top. Except for losing the knife, it was a perfect leap.

He dropped to the ground, landed running, and didn't quit until his breath came in such painful gasps that he thought his chest would burst if he didn't stop.

After that, everything went his way.

The clothesline was an incredible piece of luck. He had planned to look for a do-it-yourself laundromat near one of the motels on the outskirts of town. People often put their clothes in the machines and leave them unattended while they go somewhere to eat or shop. He could help himself from one of the clothes dryers.

But as he walked toward the city, staying in the ditch of the old, seldom-used road that had long since been made obsolete by a freeway, he saw a white farmhouse. In the yard, rows of clothes fluttered dry in the breeze.

He circled the house and approached it from behind. A shaggy yellow dog barked once from the back porch; Tony flattened himself in the grass.

The dog came closer, its ears back.

"Go away," Tony hissed. "Scram! Get out of here."

The dog gave a low growl. Tony hated animals and they always seemed to sense his feelings and return them.

In the grass, his finger closed around a small stone. Tony flung the stone at the dog. It hit the top of the dog's head and bounced off. The dog yelped. It turned, put its tail between its legs, and slunk back to the porch.

Tony stayed low in the grass a few minutes, in case someone came to see why the dog had barked. His ears strained to hear possible footsteps.

Nothing.

Slowly, he raised his head and looked in all directions. The dog was curled up beside the back door; it appeared to be asleep. Tony saw no one and heard nothing. He stood and walked quickly to the clothesline. He jerked the clothespins loose with one hand and grabbed the clothes with the other. A faded pair of overalls. A bright red shirt. A khaki jacket.

Later, when he was safely away from the house, he hid in a clump of bushes and changed into his new clothes. The sleeves of the red shirt were an inch too long, so he rolled them partway up. The overalls were a bit big, too, but overalls are always loose fitting. The length was just right. Whoever owned those overalls must be very close to Tony's height of six feet one inch.

He found a large rock, dug a hole in the dirt beside it, and put his prison clothes in the hole. Then he sat on the ground and, using his feet, pushed the rock over the hole.

Dressed in his red shirt and overalls, with the khaki jacket tied around his waist, Tony returned to the road.

This time he didn't stay low. He hiked in plain sight along the shoulder and when he heard a vehicle approach, he boldly put out his thumb.

An old pickup whizzed past, then slammed on its brakes and backed up. A young man, seventeen or eighteen years old, was driving; two girls of about the same age were with him. The girls giggled as they looked at Tony.

"How far are you going?" Tony asked.

"Seattle," the driver said. "If you don't mind riding in the back end, hop in." The girls giggled again.

Tony put one foot on the back bumper and swung his leg over the tailgate. It was perfect. He could lie down, where nobody could see him. And he didn't have to talk to anyone, didn't have to make up a story about who he was or where he came from or where he was going. By tomorrow, the kids in the pickup wouldn't even remember what he looked like.

The truck roared off again. Tony cushioned his head on his arms and tried to brace himself when the truck hit rough spots. Soon the bumpiness ended and, peering over the top of the truck bed, Tony saw they had reached the freeway on-ramp. It was smooth riding all the way to Seattle.

At the first red light after the truck had left the freeway, Tony hopped out. The three people in the pickup were putting a new tape in the tape deck. They didn't notice when he left.

Two hours later, Tony slipped the knife up the sleeve of his jacket and walked out of the secondhand store.

He had dreamed of this day for months, ever since he was convicted of armed robbery. No way was Tony

11

Haymes going to stay locked in prison. Forget it. Old Tony had plans for his life and they didn't include years behind bars. No way.

This time, the cops wouldn't find him. This time, luck was with him. First the clothes. Then those kids in the pickup. And now the knife. Everything was going exactly the way he had hoped. Even better. September tenth was definitely his lucky day.

He walked briskly away from the secondhand store. Next he needed to find a safe place to spend the night. Not a room. Even if he had money to rent a room, he didn't want to talk to any room clerk.

A park bench would do, or a tree to lie under. The weather was mild for September and it wouldn't be the first time Tony had slept all night on the ground. But it had to be someplace where he could be sure no cop would come nosing around. The last thing he needed was for a cop to think he was a drunken wino and try to take him in.

Tony sauntered up the street, sizing up doorways, watching for back alleys.

Ahead, a large sign said, WOODLAND PARK ZOO. Bingo.

That's where he would spend the night. A zoo would have dozens of hiding places and no people around at night.

He crossed the zoo parking lot and watched the entrance. Three elderly women bought tickets and went in.

Tony frowned. The ticket booths were the only entrances and he didn't have any money. Brick walls extended on either side of the booths and when the wall ended, chain link fence began.

A group of schoolchildren and their teacher came out of the zoo through an exit turnstile. The turnstile was like a revolving door and the kids laughed and hollered as they tried to see how fast they could push it.

Rowdy little monsters, Tony thought. They reminded him of the kid who had tipped off the cops and got Tony arrested. Who would have guessed that a ten-year-old boy, watching out his bedroom window, would get the license plate number of Tony's car and turn him in? If it hadn't been for that lousy kid, Tony would never have done time. Tony hated kids even more than he hated animals.

Well, his time in prison was finished now and they'd never catch Tony Haymes again. Never.

A bus pulled up and forty or fifty people got off. On the side of the bus large green letters spelled out, CLASS ACT TOURS. The people all wore round green buttons. A man in a green jacket headed straight for the ticket booth. The other people milled around, talking and reading colorful brochures.

"This way, please," the man in the green jacket called. "The zoo closes in just two hours, so we need to hurry." He went through the gate and the people in the group trailed after him.

And that's when Tony saw it, lying right on the curb beside the tour bus: one of the round green buttons. Trying to look casual, he strolled toward the bus, picked up the button, and walked away. The button said, Class

Act Tours. As he hurried toward the gate, he pinned the button on the front of his overalls.

The woman in the ticket booth didn't pay any attention to him as he followed the rest of the group into the zoo. She only looked at his Class Act Tours button.

Once inside, it was easy to leave the group. They were busy consulting their maps of the zoo and deciding which way to go first. No one noticed Tony, as he slipped away.

The Indian summer sun glowed golden through the leaves as Tony walked past the Elephant Forest, the Feline House, and the African Savanna.

I did it, he thought triumphantly. I'm free. There wasn't a cop in the world who would look for him in the zoo.

3

ELLEN looked at the clock again. "Where *are* they?" she said, as she walked to the window for the third time in five minutes. "Even if traffic was bad, they should have been here by now."

"What if their plane crashed?" Corey said. "Or maybe it was hijacked." He began to talk fast, the way he always did when he was excited by some story he was making up. "What if the plane took off on time and then a band of terrorists threatened to blow everyone up if the pilot didn't fly them all to—" Corey hesitated, trying to decide the worst possible place.

"Stop it," said Ellen. "You sound like you want Mom and Dad to get hijacked."

"I would have them escape," Corey said. "I would have them trick the hijackers and save all the people and get their pictures in the paper. Besides, it was just a story."

Ellen sighed. Her brother was always making up stories; the least little thing set him off. Her parents were sure he was going to be a famous writer some day.

She snapped on the television. That was the trouble with Corey's stories. They always seemed plausible. There was just enough truth in them to make people think that the events he described might really have happened.

She flipped from channel to channel. If an airplane headed for Seattle had been hijacked, the TV stations would be covering the story. Reporters would be broadcasting from the airport. Instead, there were the usual talk shows. Relieved, she turned the TV off.

"I'm going to call the airport and see if the plane landed on time," she said. She took her parents' itinerary off the kitchen bulletin board and read which airline and flight number.

"I'm sorry," she was told, "that flight has been delayed. I'm not sure what time it will arrive."

Ellen hung up. "Their plane isn't in yet," she said.

"But what about the zoo?" Corey cried. "Mrs. Caruthers will be waiting for us." He plopped down on the sofa and socked one of the pillows. "Mom and Dad should have come home sooner," he said. "Grandpa shouldn't have taken Grandma to the doctor today."

"It isn't Mom and Dad's fault if their plane doesn't arrive on time," Ellen said, "and Grandma can't help it that her leg hurt."

Corey punched the pillow again.

Two weeks ago, Grandma broke her leg; she was in a cast. Grandma and Grandpa had still come to stay while Mr. and Mrs. Streater were in San Francisco, but they couldn't do the camp-out. It was hard for Grandma to get around on her crutches and sleeping in a tent was out of the question.

Since Grandpa didn't want to do the camp-out without Grandma, Ellen's parents had rearranged their schedule to catch an earlier flight. They were supposed to be home in time to pick up Ellen and Corey and get to the zoo by five.

That's when they were supposed to meet Mrs. Caruthers, the representative of the zoological society. She would have their picnic supper and would show them the tent where they were going to sleep.

Ellen looked at the clock again. It was almost 4:30. She wondered what her parents would want them to do.

Corey's bottom lip trembled. "We're going to miss the camp-out," he said.

I'm the adult, Ellen thought. I have to be mature, to take charge. "We'll go to the zoo," she said. "Mom and Dad know what time we're supposed to be there. They'll probably assume that Grandpa will drive us to the zoo and they'll go straight to the zoo from the airport. We'll take their sleeping bags with us and meet them there."

"How are we going to get there? It's too late to take a bus."

"Maybe Mr. Zither will drive us." Mr. Zither was the Streaters' next-door neighbor.

"Mr. Zither isn't home. I saw him leave."

Ellen dialed Mr. Zither's number, just in case he had returned. There was no answer.

"I told you he wasn't home," Corey said, as Ellen hung

17

up the phone. "How come nobody ever believes me?"

Because you're always telling stories, Ellen thought. But all she said was, "I'm going to call a cab."

Corey hopped off the sofa and threw the pillow in the air. "Get one of the limousine cabs," he said. "A white one. They're about a hundred feet long. When we drive up, everyone will stare and think we're TV actors. Maybe someone will ask me for my autograph."

"Limos are too expensive," Ellen said.

After she called the cab, she took money, to pay the cab driver, from the "emergency envelope" that her mother kept in a kitchen drawer. She had never taken money from it before but she felt sure she was doing the right thing. Grandma and Grandpa had spent several hundred dollars for the zoo camp-out, and Mrs. Caruthers was waiting for them. It would be terrible not to show up.

She hoped she was guessing correctly that her parents would go straight to the zoo. What if they didn't? They might think that Grandpa would go on the camp-out, in which case they would come home to be with Grandma, instead of going to the zoo.

Prince whined and sat by the door.

"Take Prince out, while I leave a note," Ellen said. "Grandma and Grandpa will probably eat dinner out after they see the doctor. They might not get back until late."

While Corey took Prince outside, Ellen wrote a note, just in case her parents came home instead of going directly to the zoo.

Dear Mom and Dad:

We are waiting for you at the zoo. We have your sleeping bags. We took a cab because Grandma had trouble with her cast and Grandpa took her to the doctor to have it checked. Grandma says to have fun on the camp-out and not to worry about her.

Love,
Ellen

She placed the note on top of the telephone answering machine. Her parents always checked the answering machine as soon as they got home, to see if there were any messages. Ellen believed her parents would go straight to the zoo from the airport, but if they didn't, they would find her note and go to the zoo then.

As Corey and Prince came in the back door, the cab honked in front of the house. Corey dashed outside. Ellen gathered sleeping bags in her arms, locked the front door, and left.

Mrs. Caruthers was pacing outside the zoo's south gate, where they were supposed to meet her, when the cab pulled up. "Thank heaven you're here," she cried. "Just before I left home to come to meet you, I had a call from my son-in-law. My daughter has gone to the hospital to have her baby."

Ellen paid the driver and he helped them unload their sleeping bags.

"Where are your parents?" Mrs. Caruthers asked.

"They'll meet us here," Ellen said. "Their flight from San Francisco was late."

"Oh," Mrs. Caruthers said. "Oh, dear." She bit her bottom lip. "The tent is all set up for you, in the North Meadow. I was hoping . . ."

"You don't need to stay with us," Ellen said. "We'll wait inside the gate for Mom and Dad and we know where the North Meadow is. We've been to the zoo lots of times."

"I can't leave you here alone," Mrs. Caruthers said.

"Mom and Dad will be here any minute," Ellen said.

"Maybe your daughter will have twins," Corey said. Mrs. Caruthers's eyes widened. "Maybe even triplets! If she has triplets, she'll win lots of prizes, like diaper service and cases of baby food. She might even get her picture in the paper, with all her babies."

"This is my first grandchild," Mrs. Caruthers said. She sounded a trifle breathless.

"Then you should hurry along to the hospital," Ellen said. "We don't want you to miss the birth of your grandchild—"

"Or grandchildren," Corey interjected.

"Because of us," Ellen finished.

"I'll have someone else wait with you until your parents arrive." Mrs. Caruthers led the way to the ticket booth. "Your tent is on the far side of the North Meadow," she said. "I'll get a map for you from the ticket booth."

"We don't need a map," Corey said. "The North Meadow's that way." He pointed. "The monkeys are that way, and . . ."

"There are flashlights in the tent, and a first-aid kit and an ice chest containing your picnic supper."

"I hope there's plenty of dessert," said Corey.

Ellen poked him in the ribs with her elbow and said, "Shh."

"The night security guard will pass the North Meadow around midnight and again at three. If you need anything, he'll help." She stopped at the ticket booth. "These are the campers," she said to the woman in the booth, as Ellen and Corey proceeded into the zoo. The ticket seller nodded without looking up from the novel she was reading. "They're going to wait here with you until their parents arrive."

Mrs. Caruthers stepped inside the ticket booth and picked up the telephone. "I'll call the zoo office," she said to Ellen and Corey, "so they know what's happened."

"Here come Mom and Dad!" cried Corey.

"Thank goodness," said Mrs. Caruthers, as she hung up the phone.

"Where?" said Ellen.

"There," said Corey, as he pointed to the far left side of the parking lot. "They just drove in. They're parking the car over there, behind that bus."

"In that case," said Mrs. Caruthers, "I'll be on my way. Tell your parents I'm sorry I had to rush off." She patted the ticket person's shoulder. "We don't need your help, after all," she said.

"We'll read the paper tomorrow," Corey said, "in case it's twins. Or triplets."

Mrs. Caruthers gulped. "Have a wonderful time tonight," she said, as she turned and dashed toward the right end of the parking lot. Seconds later, she drove out of the lot.

"You shouldn't have upset Mrs. Caruthers like that,"

Ellen said. "She's probably worried enough about her daughter, without you cackling about twins."

Corey looked innocent. "Maybe her daughter *will* have twins," he said. "Or triplets."

"People who are going to have more than one baby know it ahead of time," Ellen said.

"Always?"

"Almost always." Ellen peered across the rows of cars in the parking lot. "I don't see Mom and Dad," she said.

Corey looked at his shoes and didn't answer.

Ellen scowled at her brother. "Corey Streater! Did you make that up, about seeing them?"

Corey put his finger to his lips. He took Ellen's arm and led her away from the ticket booth. "Mrs. Caruthers was going to put that dopey ticket lady in charge of us," he whispered.

"You lied to Mrs. Caruthers."

"She really wanted to go," Corey said. "I just made it so she wouldn't feel bad about leaving us. And Mom and Dad will get here any minute. You said so yourself."

"Still, it was wrong to pretend you saw them."

Corey hung his head. "I guess it was," he admitted. "I'm sorry."

"You should be."

Straight ahead was a partially enclosed viewing area where the zoo visitors could watch the African animals. Ellen and Corey carried their gear to a wooden bench and sat down. "We might as well watch the animals while we wait for Mom and Dad," Ellen said. "We can take turns going back to the gate, so we don't miss them."

"Let's look through the telescopes," Corey said, pointing at one of the coin-operated metal telescopes that were mounted on each side of the enclosure.

"They cost a quarter and I don't have any money."

"Didn't you get change from the cab?"

"I let the driver keep it. You're supposed to tip the cab driver."

"Look," Corey cried. "Giraffes! Maybe the giraffes sprout wings at night and fly all around the zoo and we'll jump on their backs and ride them."

For once Corey's wild imagination didn't irritate her. She was too excited about spending the night at the zoo to be bothered by her brother. Except for his storytelling, he wasn't so bad, for an eight year old. By the time he was mature, like her, maybe he would learn to control his tall tales.

A small child began crying and Ellen went back to the entrance area to see what was wrong. It was a little girl who didn't want to leave the zoo. Her parents kept telling her they'd come again another day but the child sobbed as they carried her through the exit turnstile.

Quite a few people were leaving. Three old women. A young couple. A whole group of people wearing green buttons that said, Class Act Tours. A man in a green jacket hurried the tour group along, calling, "The zoo is closed! The bus leaves in five minutes."

Ellen glanced at the entry again. The ticket booth was empty. She looked out toward the parking area. There was no sign of her parents.

"Maybe they won't show," Corey said. "Maybe their plane crashed and . . ."

"Stop it!"

" . . . and they were the only survivors who weren't hurt and they can't call us because they're busy helping the injured. Mom and Dad will be heroes and get their pictures in the paper."

Ellen had noticed that Corey's stories often ended with the person getting his or her picture in the newspaper.

She wondered whether to wait where they were or go to the North Meadow where they were supposed to camp. She decided to wait awhile longer. Surely her parents would arrive at any moment.

A giraffe nibbled hay that hung from a strap, high in a tree. It always astonished her that such large animals were so graceful. She gazed up at the long, slender neck. *How beautiful you are*, she thought.

The giraffe quit eating and looked down at Ellen. Was it possible that the giraffe had received her message? Without planning to, had she communicated with an animal besides Prince? Maybe she could experiment with the zoo animals while she was here. That would add a new dimension to her science project.

She looked up, directly into the giraffe's big brown eyes. *How beautiful you are.*

"Ellen! Come quick!" Corey's excited cry came from around the corner, out of sight.

She left the enclosed viewing area and hurried along the path toward the sound of his voice. She found him standing on a big rock, pointing in delight. "The zebras," he said, "are doing the hula."

Ellen looked. Two zebras stood in the field, swishing their tails and moving their rear ends back and forth. Probably trying to get rid of flies, Ellen thought.

"At night," Corey said, "all the animals dance. When there are no people watching, all the zebras do the hula. And the bears boogie."

Ellen giggled. Maybe her parents were right; maybe Corey would be a writer some day.

While Ellen watched the zebras wiggle their rear ends, Corey jumped off the rock and disappeared again. Soon he came dashing back. "I found Hugo," he said. "He's just around the corner."

She followed him along the path toward the Elephant Forest.

"There he is," Corey said. "That's him, all right."

Corey was right. The African elephant that they had helped bathe was standing at the edge of the Elephant Forest. Hugo was the zoo's oldest elephant: fifty-nine years old, the same age as Ellen's grandma. They had joked about that with Grandma while they washed him.

"Let's see if we can make Hugo purr," Corey said.

The elephants' trainer had told them that elephants sometimes purr, just the way cats do. "They do it when they're content," the trainer had said, "when they're with someone they trust. It's a low, rumbling purr and you might not be able to hear it."

The trainer also said Hugo liked music. He sang a song to Hugo, hoping to make Hugo purr for Ellen and Corey. Hugo seemed to like the song but he hadn't purred.

Together, Corey and Ellen crossed the path and got as close to the elephant area as they could.

"Hey, Hugo," Corey called. "Some of the zebras learned to hula and they're going to Hollywood to star in a movie."

Hugo rubbed his side against the fence.

Ellen blotted out the sound of Corey's voice and focused all her thoughts on the big elephant.

Hello, Hugo, she said in her mind. *I am your friend. I am glad to see you. You are a magnificent elephant.*

Hugo turned his head and looked at Ellen. His trunk reached out toward her, sniffing the air. His wide ears were flat on either side of his head, like giant wings waiting to spread. Ellen suppressed a giggle. Maybe it's the elephants, not the giraffes, that fly around at night, she thought. Like Dumbo.

"Is he doing it?" Corey said. "Can you hear any purring?"

Ellen heard nothing. But the elephant *did* seem to be staring at her. Was he just curious? Could he possibly remember them, from when they gave him a bath nearly two years ago? Or had he somehow received Ellen's mental message?

She beamed it again. *We are glad to see you, elephant friend.*

"I think he remembers us," Corey said. "Wow! Wait until Mom and Dad hear about this."

The mention of their parents reminded Ellen that they were supposed to be watching the gate. "Come on," she said. "We have to stay by the gate. We don't want to miss Mom and Dad."

She checked the entrance area and then returned to the bench, disappointed to see that the giraffe had moved on. Corey kept wandering down the path, trying to see where the dancing zebras were. Finally, to keep him in sight,

Ellen suggested that they take the sleeping bags to the North Meadow and leave them in the tent.

"Maybe Mom and Dad are already there," Corey said. "If they got here just as the zoo was closing, maybe they went in a different gate and they're waiting for us by the tent."

Ellen didn't point out that Mom and Dad had no way to know where the tent was.

They passed the Family Farm area, where children are allowed to pet donkeys, pigs, and sheep. They passed the orangutans and the gorillas. They passed the Nocturnal House, Ellen's favorite zoo exhibit.

It was always dark inside the Nocturnal House, and visitors stood on the walkway surrounded by glass walls. After their eyes adjusted to the darkness, they could look through the glass to the dimly lit treetops on the other side where owls sat, and possums hung by their tails, and giant bats slowly unfolded their wings. When Ellen was in the Nocturnal House, she always felt as if she were hiding in the trees and spying on the nocturnal animals through a secret peephole.

"We'll still stay, won't we?" Corey said. "Even if Mom and Dad don't come?"

"I don't know." Ellen wasn't quite ready to deal with that possibility.

"We have to," Corey said. "I bet a kid in my class that I was going to spend all night at the zoo tonight and if I don't do it, I'll lose ten dollars."

"Ten dollars! Why did you make such a big bet? Why didn't you bet a nickel or a dime?"

"Because I knew I would win." He kicked a pebble and sent it skittering down the path ahead of them. "I don't even have ten dollars," he admitted. "I'll have it on Monday, though, when I win the bet. I should have tried to bet with a whole bunch of kids. If lots of kids had bet that I wasn't sleeping at the zoo tonight, I could collect tons of money on Monday." They caught up with the pebble and he kicked it again. "I should have tried to bet with at least twenty kids. Maybe even thirty."

"I doubt there are twenty kids in your school who would be stupid enough to make a ten-dollar bet," Ellen said, as they approached the North Meadow.

Corey spotted the tent. "There it is," he yelled, as he dropped the two sleeping bags he was carrying and dashed across the meadow. Seconds later, he emerged from the tent, calling, "They aren't in here."

Ellen had known they wouldn't be. When Mom and Dad got to the zoo, they would come to the south gate, as instructed, even if it was late.

She bent to pick up the sleeping bags that Corey had dropped. As she did, she glimpsed a flash of red through the trees. For an instant, she thought it was a person, someone wearing a red coat or a red shirt. But when she turned to get a better look, no one was there.

Probably a red leaf, Ellen thought. A bright autumn leaf, falling from one of the trees.

4

DUSK settled over the meadow. A single star glimmered low in the darkening sky.

Star light, star bright, first star I've seen tonight. The old chant ran through Ellen's mind. *I wish I may, I wish I might, have the wish I wish tonight.*

She closed her eyes briefly. *I wish Mom and Dad would get here.*

She opened the flap of the tent and peeked in. Corey was rummaging in the ice chest.

"Sandwiches," he announced. "And apples and brownies. Let's eat the brownies first."

"We can eat later," she said. "We need to get back to the gate so we don't miss Mom and Dad. They're probably waiting for us."

"What if they aren't there?"

"If they aren't, we'll call Grandpa and Grandma."

"They won't make us come home, will they?"

She knew he was worried about his ten-dollar bet. "I have no idea what they'll say," she said, although she was certain that her grandparents would do exactly that. Most likely, Grandpa and Grandma would come immediately and take them home. Unless Corey could talk Grandpa into staying here overnight and leaving Grandma home by herself. She was sure Corey would try.

"Where are you going to find a telephone?"

"I saw one when we came. It's just on the other side of the ticket booth, near where the taxi stopped."

They started back, past the Nocturnal House. "I want to go in the marsh," Corey said, "and see where the cranes sleep."

Ellen hesitated. The marsh, she knew, was at the corner of the zoo, near the parking lot. She supposed they could go that way and then take the outside path back to the entrance. It wouldn't be much out of the way.

When they reached the Family Farm, they left the main path and went toward the marsh. As they drew near the Animal Health Care building, Ellen thought she heard voices.

She ran to the building and tried the door. It was locked. She knocked loudly. No one came. She stood there for a moment, listening and waiting, but she heard nothing more.

"Hurry up," Corey said. "Maybe the cranes play secret games at night, like duck, duck, gray duck or wingtip tag."

When they reached the first of the wire doors that led into the marsh area, it was locked.

"We can't go in," Corey wailed. "Somebody locked the door."

"Probably the security guard," Ellen said. Somehow she felt better, knowing the guard was at the zoo, taking care of his duties.

Instead of taking the outer path, Ellen retraced her steps and led Corey past the Animal Health Care building again. She could swear she had heard someone talking there. She knocked at the door again. There was no answer.

"The light is out now," Corey said.

"What light?"

"Before when we were here, I could see light under the door. Now I can't."

Then someone *had* been inside. More than one person, if she'd heard voices. Why hadn't they come to the door when she knocked?

"Cross your fingers that Mom and Dad are waiting for us," she said.

As they approached the entrance area, Corey said, "Let's tell Mom and Dad that they missed all the excitement. Let's say a buffalo got loose and it was stampeding down this path, right toward our tent. And you and I waved our arms and got its attention and then we talked to it and got it all calmed down and put it back where it belongs."

Ellen agreed, knowing Corey would do it whether she said yes or not.

31

Corey didn't get to tell his buffalo story.

As they approached the zoo entrance, Ellen could see that no one was there. She tried not to let Corey see her disappointment. When she made the decision to come to the zoo alone, she had been certain that Mom and Dad would arrive shortly. Now she was no longer sure that she had done the right thing.

"It's lucky for us I always carry money for a phone call," Ellen said. She took off her left shoe and pulled on the piece of tape that kept the quarter from sliding around.

"You said you didn't have any money," Corey complained.

"This is for emergency phone calls only. Mom told me that when she put it in my shoe."

She put her shoe back on, stood up, and followed Corey toward the entrance walkway.

At exactly the same instant, they saw it. Metal fencing completely blocked both the ticket booth walkways where people entered the zoo. The fencing had been lowered from the ceiling. Ellen peered through the fencing at the telephone.

"We could go out the exit turnstile and call," Corey said, "but how would we get back in?"

"We won't. But we have to call and tell Grandma and Grandpa that Mom and Dad haven't come."

"Maybe we can climb backward through the turnstile," Corey said.

They walked to the right, toward the turnstile. When they reached it, Ellen stopped and stared. The turnstile was also blocked by a heavy metal gate.

"It must slide into place after everyone has left for the night," Ellen said.

Corey pushed on the gate but it didn't budge. "It's locked," he said. "Mom and Dad can't get in."

And we can't get out, Ellen thought. Where were her parents? Even with a delayed flight, they should have reached the zoo by now. Had Corey's terrible story been a premonition? Had the plane been hijacked? Had it crashed and burned?

She pushed the negative thoughts out of her mind. Her mother always said there was no point worrying because 99 percent of the things we worry about never happen.

"What if Mom and Dad came and they couldn't get in so they went home?" Corey said.

"If they did, they found our note and know where we are and they'll make arrangements to get in. They're probably calling someone from the zoo right now."

"Mrs. Caruthers isn't home," Corey said. "Too bad."

He didn't sound like he thought it was too bad. He sounded like he was glad his parents might have a hard time getting into the zoo.

Ellen frowned at him. He was probably concocting all sorts of wild stories about what happened during the zoo night camp-out. When his friends found out that his parents weren't here, they would believe anything Corey made up.

As if to confirm Ellen's suspicions, Corey added, "Mom and Dad would make us go to sleep. This way we can stay up all night and have lots of adventures."

"Aren't you even worried about Mom and Dad?" Ellen said crossly.

Corey shrugged. "We can't do anything about it, so why waste time worrying?"

She couldn't argue with his logic.

"The security guard must have a telephone," Ellen said. "I wonder where his office is."

"I don't know. Let's go eat; I'm starving."

Ellen agreed. There must be other telephones; maybe they would find one on their way to the tent. If not, it would be best to stay there and watch for the security guard. They would tell him what had happened. He knew someone was camping in the meadow so he might even come before midnight.

Ellen's stomach growled. Since she and Corey were apparently going to spend at least part of the night alone in the zoo, they might as well go ahead and enjoy the picnic.

It was dark now. Even with her flashlight on, Ellen could see only a few feet ahead of her. The giant trees that were so magnificent in the sunlight, now seemed twisted and sinister.

Ellen shivered. She wished she hadn't left her sweater in the tent. She wished she could find a telephone. Most of all, she wished she had stayed home.

"Let's take the path the other way," Corey said. "We'll still come to the tent and we might see mountain goats tap-dancing. We can stand on the big rocks and the flashlight can be our spotlight, like we're in a theater."

Ellen wondered how Corey could be so unconcerned about their plight. How could he think about dancing goats when they were locked in the zoo all alone?

"It's much longer to walk that way," she said. "We're going straight back to the tent."

"After they tap-dance, they'll do ballet."

"Sure they will. The ducks are probably doing *Swan Lake* right now."

Corey missed her sarcastic tone. "Maybe the mountain goats will fly, too." He grinned at her. "What if ALL the animals sprout wings at night and nobody knows it?" He put his hand in his armpits and, moving his elbows up and down like wings, he galloped down the path.

I might as well talk to the moon, Ellen thought, as she shook her head and started after him. Dancing zebras. Flying goats. What would he think of next?

Moments later, Corey rushed back to her. "Somebody's up there," he whispered, pointing at the path ahead. "And he's trying to break into the little store."

"It's the security person that Mrs. Caruthers told us about. Good. He's probably making sure everything is locked properly." She was glad they had found the security guard. He would take them to a telephone. Maybe he even carried a portable phone with him.

Corey grabbed her arm, forcing her to stop walking. "He isn't checking the locks," he insisted. "He has a tool in his hand and he's trying to pry open a window."

Ellen scowled. "If this is one of your stories and you're trying to scare me, you'd better quit right now," she said.

"No! It's true, I swear it."

Something in Corey's voice made her believe him.

"Where is he?" she whispered. "How far ahead of us?"

"Across from the Elephant Forest. It's the snack shop where we bought popcorn last time we came."

"Did he see you?"

Corey shook his head, no.

"You're sure?"

"Positive. I saw him from behind and I didn't make any noise. I came to tell you right away."

Ellen turned and started in the other direction. "We're going back to our tent," she said.

Corey didn't follow her.

"Come on," she hissed.

"I'm going to spy on the zoo man," he said.

"What? Don't be an idiot."

"Maybe he's a crook. Maybe he steals things from the zoo at night and nobody knows it. If we see him do it, we can tell Mrs. Caruthers." The words came faster. "The police will ask us questions. We'll be detectives. We'll be heroes! We'll get our pictures in the paper."

"If he's a crook, we're going to keep out of his way. Now, come with me."

Corey stayed where he was. "Dad always says when someone is doing something wrong, people should take a stand. He says everyone is scared to get involved."

Ellen hesitated. Corey was right; Dad did say that.

"The zoo man won't see us," Corey said. "We'll stay on the other side of the path. There are trees and bushes to hide in. All we have to do is watch, to see what he does. That's all. And then tomorrow morning we can tell Mrs. Caruthers what we saw."

Ellen switched her flashlight off. Silently, they rounded the curve in the path, staying close to the right-hand edge, near the rhododendrons. As they came to a cleared area that contained a picnic table, Corey stopped and pointed.

Ellen squinted in the dim light. On the other side of the path, about fifty feet ahead, she could make out the dark outline of a building. She knew it was the food building, where her family often bought a treat when they visited the zoo.

She heard a noise like someone hammering lightly on wood. When her eyes focused in the direction of the noise, she saw the outline of a man. He stood at the side of the building, beside the wooden panels which open to make a pass-through counter.

More noise. Corey was right. The man was breaking into the food stand. The panel was probably easier to force open than the door.

Ellen, with Corey beside her, crouched low beside the bushes and watched. She couldn't see exactly what the man was doing but she saw movement and she heard the wooden panel creak.

A light went on inside the food stand. The panel was raised up and hooked to the roof overhang. Through the opening, she could see him clearly now as he pulled out drawers and slammed them shut again. He picked up a bag of potato chips, ripped off one end, and began to eat.

"Details," whispered Corey.

Ellen put her finger to her mouth, warning him to keep quiet. She knew what he meant, though. For awhile, Corey's stories had centered on a make-believe detective who always astounded the police by remembering every detail of the villain's description.

Ellen stared at the man. He looked tall, although it was

hard to be sure when she was crouched so low. Six feet probably. Maybe even taller. Dark hair. A khaki jacket. Jeans.

The man turned, still searching the inside of the food stand. His jacket was open. Ellen saw a red shirt. And it wasn't jeans, it was overalls. Bib overalls. Wouldn't the security guard wear a uniform?

The man stopped moving. He picked up a small box, held it toward the light, and examined it. He laid the box on the counter and bent over it. Something glinted in the light from the bare bulb inside the food stand.

Corey clutched her arm.

The man had a knife. A big knife. He was using it to break open the lock on the box.

That's probably what he used to pry open the panel, too, Ellen thought.

He lifted the lid of the box and reached inside.

Money. He removed a stack of bills and began counting them.

Corey leaned closer and she was afraid he was going to say something. She put her finger to her lips again. The whites of Corey's eyes seemed enormous as he pointed at the man.

Ellen nodded. She watched as the man put the bills in the pocket of his jacket and zipped the pocket shut. Then he calmly sat on the counter of the food stand and continued to eat potato chips.

Ellen dropped to her hands and knees and began to crawl away from the food stand, staying as close as possible to the bushes. She was afraid to stand up, since the man was facing in their direction. Even though they were far beyond the rectangle of light that fell from the open panel to the ground outside, she didn't want to take any chance that he would see movement and come to investigate.

Glancing over her shoulder, she saw that Corey was creeping along too, directly behind her. When they rounded the curve, heading back toward the south gate, Ellen stood up.

Corey stood beside her and slipped his hand in hers. For once, he kept his mouth shut. Ellen took a deep breath and then jogged toward the gorilla house, back to the North Meadow and the safety of their tent.

The moon rose silently, sending a dim light over the zoo. Ellen looked up. The moon was nearly full. A harvest moon, her mother would call it. In her mind, she could hear Mom singing, as she always did when they sat together around a campfire: "Shine on, Shine on, harvest moon, up in the sky."

Mom. Where are you? Why haven't you come?

Ellen wished she had not brought Corey to the zoo. It had seemed right at the time but she had been positive her parents would join them. She hadn't counted on being locked in the zoo alone with Corey all night.

And she certainly hadn't counted on discovering that a thief was prowling around the zoo.

5

"I'M GOING to spy on him some more," Corey said.

"No, you aren't. We're both staying right here in this tent."

They were sitting on their sleeping bags, with the picnic supper between them. There were chicken salad sandwiches, ham and cheese sandwiches, little bags of chips, apples, bananas, and chocolate-frosted brownies. There were cans of apple juice, too, and even a little bag of after-dinner mints.

The basket contained enough for four people, but after nibbling at half a sandwich, Ellen quit. Despite her grumbling stomach and the delicious food, nothing tasted good. She was too nervous to eat.

"We need to gather all the evidence we can," Corey said. "Maybe the security guard does other bad stuff."

"I don't think that man was the guard."

"Then who was it?"

"I don't know. But we'll find out what the guard looks like when he comes past here at midnight. You can spy on him then, from inside the tent. If he isn't the thief, we can tell him what we saw."

"I don't want to tell the guard. I want to be a detective and gather more evidence."

"We don't need more evidence and it would make him angry if he caught us following him."

Corey bit into another brownie. "Well, I'm not staying in this dumb tent all night. I want to walk around the zoo. What good is it to spend the night in the zoo if we don't see anything but the inside of a tent? I want to have an adventure."

"You'll have more of an adventure than you bargain for if that thief catches you spying on him."

"He won't catch me."

"That's right. He won't catch you because you aren't going to do it."

A loud roar from across the meadow made both of them jump.

"A lion," Corey said.

"Be quiet and listen. Maybe we can hear some of the other animals."

They stretched out on top of their sleeping bags and listened.

The lion roared again, a deep throaty noise that ended on a high whine. Ellen closed her eyes and strained her ears to hear more. All was quiet.

It felt cozy in the tent, the way it felt when her family went camping. Outside the tent, there was only silence. Gradually, her tight muscles relaxed.

41

Ellen took a deep breath and then another.
The silence stretched on.

———

ELLEN and Corey's grandparents squinted at the X ray as
the doctor held it in front of the light.

"I'm sorry, Mrs. Howard," the doctor said. "The leg
is not healing properly. I'm afraid we'll have to reset it."

"Now? Tonight?"

"The sooner the better. I've already called the hospital
and arranged to have you admitted."

"But—"

"You may as well get it over with tonight, Esther,"
Grandpa said. "You don't want to limp the rest of your
life."

"If you like, you can spend the night at the hospital,
too, Mr. Howard," the doctor said. "We have several
sleeping rooms for relatives to use in cases like this, when
we do unplanned surgery at night."

"Yes," Grandpa said. "Yes, I'll do that."

"We'd better call the children," Grandma said, "and
make sure Mike and Dorothy got home. We can't leave
Corey and Ellen there by themselves."

"Use my phone, if you like," the doctor said.

Grandpa dialed. He waited a moment and then said,
"I got the answering machine. That means they've gone
on the camp-out."

He waited until the machine made a little *bleep* and
then said, "Hello, it's me. Esther and I are on our way

to the hospital. She has to have her leg reset and I'm going to stay at the hospital tonight, in case she needs me. I'll call you tomorrow, after you get home from the zoo."

When he hung up, Grandma said, "I'm glad Mike and Dorothy got home in time. I was afraid the plane might be late and Ellen and Corey would have to miss the camp-out."

Grandpa said, "You worry too much."

COREY'S eyes felt heavy. He struggled to keep them open. No matter what Ellen said, he didn't want to waste his night at the zoo by falling asleep. Maybe if he walked around awhile, he wouldn't feel so tired.

"I have to go to the bathroom," he whispered.

There was no response.

"Ellen?"

Ellen was asleep. Quietly, Corey got up from his sleeping bag. He put two apples in his jacket pockets. He found his flashlight, his camera, and the bag of peanuts that he had brought along, in case he got hungry in the night. He slipped through the flap of the tent and started off in the moonlight.

After he went to the bathroom, he would take the long way back to the tent. He would go past the snow leopards and the other big cats. Maybe one of them would roar at him.

Yes. That's what he would do. Heck, if he was going to be at the zoo all night, he had to have some fun. Let

Ellen sleep in the tent if she wanted to. Corey would have his adventure by himself.

———

ACROSS the zoo, on the other side of the lion area, Tony Haymes walked quietly down the path. He felt good now that he had eaten and even though there had been only fifty dollars in the cashbox, it was better than having no money at all. He also had two bananas and a sandwich in his jacket pocket, along with the cash. It was always nice to know where his next meal was coming from.

He had pulled the panel securely shut and left the snack shop through the door. No one would be able to tell he had been inside the building until they opened the cashbox and found it empty.

Tony smiled. I haven't lost my touch, he thought. Eight months in prison couldn't take away talent like his. Of course, fifty bucks was peanuts compared to Tony's usual haul.

That's what I need, he decided. A big job. Fast. Make enough in a hurry to get me out of the country, let me lie low for awhile. Then I'll start over somewhere else. Mexico, maybe. He'd heard there were ways to make big bucks in Mexico. But in order to get to Mexico he had to do more than pilfer petty cash from a hot dog stand.

Think big, he told himself. Think big. Bank robbery? No. Too risky. All the banks have surveillance cameras these days and he would be recognized. Jewelry store? No. He would need a fence to get rid of the stolen goods and he was out of touch.

He left the African area behind and meandered past the orangutans and great apes. There was a special display outside the monkey house and, curious, Tony squinted in the moonlight to see what it said.

COME MEET THE NEW BABY! We are pleased to announce that a golden lion tamarin monkey was born here on August 2nd. This species seldom reproduces in captivity. The baby is healthy and enjoys having visitors.

Next to the announcement were several snapshots of a baby monkey. Tony stared at the pictures for a long time. The monkey was tiny, no bigger than a doll. In one of the pictures, a person was holding it and the little monkey had its arms wrapped around the person's neck and its head snuggled against the person's chest just the way a little child might.

There was also a newspaper article about the birth of the baby monkey. The headline said: RARE BABY MONKEY ATTRACTS ZOO VISITORS. The story began by saying zoo attendance was up 35 percent since the birth of the baby monkey.

Tony tugged on the glass doors that led inside the monkey house. They were locked. He cupped his hands on the sides of his face and peered inside.

The interior of the building was dimly lit, as if the zoo were trying to match the moonlight of the outdoors. Tony could see glass partitions which separated zoo visitors from the floor-to-ceiling chain link enclosures where the monkeys lived.

Inside the enclosures, he saw trees, fallen logs, and platforms at various heights. In one cage, high up by the ceiling, there was a swing.

Something moved in the cage closest to where he stood. Tony saw a small shape. For a moment he thought it was a squirrel. When it moved again, another, smaller, shape followed and he realized that it was the golden tamarin monkey and her famous baby.

And that's when he knew how he would get enough money to go to Mexico. He would kidnap the baby monkey and hold it for ransom.

It should be a snap. All he had to do was get into the cage and coax the little monkey to come to him. That would be simple enough.

Tony's heart began to pound as he thought of what he would do after he had the monkey. He'd get a room somewhere, hide out, and demand a ransom. The zoo must have plenty of money and if they didn't, they would get it from the public. People who love animals are suckers for animal sob stories. The public would contribute. All the people who had come to the zoo to see the baby monkey would want to help get it back. They'd give money; he was sure of it.

Twenty thousand dollars. Tony leaned his head against the cool glass door and closed his eyes. He would demand a $20,000 ransom for the return of the baby monkey. And he would get it.

But first he had to have the monkey. He squinted through the door again. Even if he broke in, the glass partitions inside looked solid and so did the chain fencing. Even his knife couldn't cut through chain like that; it would take a hacksaw.

Take your time, he told himself. Calm down and think it through before you act.

There had to be some other way to get inside. How do the keepers put food in? How are the cages cleaned? There must be some kind of entrance at the back side of each cage.

His hands dropped to his sides and he started around the outside of the monkey building. He soon came to a wooden door marked "Employees Only."

My lucky day, he told himself, as he used the knife to pick the lock on the door. As he worked, he planned his strategy. He would go through whatever opening was at the back of the rare monkey's cage. He would use the bananas in his pocket to make friends with the mother monkey. While she ate the bananas, he would pick up the baby, step back through the door or hole or whatever it was, and leave.

He would have to move quickly. Even though the monkeys were tiny, they were still wild animals and he wasn't sure what the mother would do if she saw him take her baby. The last thing he needed was to get bit.

If he had to, he would give her his sandwich, to distract her. That should keep her occupied until he and the baby were safely outside the cage.

And once he had the baby monkey? Then what? He would put the monkey inside his overalls and zip his jacket. He would take a cab—tell the driver his infant son was asleep. That would explain the lump in his coat. He would rent a motel room, one of those places where they don't ask for license numbers, just cash on the line. He had the cash, from the snack-shop box.

Tomorrow he would call the director of the zoo and tell him where and when to bring the $20,000. He would leave the monkey in the motel room, go get the money, and be on his way to Mexico.

Yes! Tony thought. It would work! Later, he could figure out exactly how to word the ransom call and arrange the pickup. Right now he needed to get the baby monkey in his jacket and get away from the zoo.

His heart thumped rapidly in his chest and little beads of moisture stood on his upper lip as he opened the "Employees Only" door and slipped silently into the area behind the monkey cages.

———

COREY paused outside the rest rooms, debating which way to go. He was tempted to head north, past the bison and wolves. He bet those wolves would be howling tonight, with the moon almost full. The thought made him shiver with excitement.

He wasn't scared. After all, what could happen to him? Still, it was odd to be here like this, in the middle of the night, with only the zoo animals.

He turned toward the lion area. The lion had roared earlier; maybe it would do so again. If not, he would keep walking, down past the orangutans and gorillas, all the way to the monkey house.

The monkey exhibits were Corey's favorite part of the zoo. Ellen liked the Nocturnal House but all those bats gave him the creeps. He'd take the monkeys any day. Monkeys were silly; they made him laugh. And it was easy to make up stories about what they did because they always did something unexpected.

He wondered if monkeys lie down to sleep at night or if they sit in the trees. Maybe they make little beds in the leaves and lie down and use each other's tails for pillows. Do monkeys dream? Do they sing monkey lullabies to their young?

Corey didn't know anything about how monkeys act at night. Well, he thought happily, this is my chance to find out.

He paused for only a moment near the lion area. When none of them roared, he decided to go on. Even with the flashlight, it wasn't as easy to find his way in the dark as he had thought it would be. He started walking toward where he thought the monkey house was.

Here I come, monkeys, he thought. You're going to have midnight company.

6

THE LION roared again.

Ellen's eyes flew open. For a moment she didn't know where she was or what she had heard. Then she remembered. She sat up, pulled the flap of the tent open, and looked out.

She wondered where her parents were. Something must have gone terribly wrong or they would be here. They would never let her and Corey spend the night here alone. Heck, she and Corey weren't even allowed to spend the night alone at home, in their own house with Prince to protect them. Grandma and Grandpa always came and stayed with them if Mom and Dad had to be gone.

"Corey?" she whispered. "Are you awake?"

There was no answer. He must be asleep. She kept still, listening for animal noises again. She heard nothing. Not even the rhythmic breathing of someone who's asleep.

She reached over toward Corey's sleeping bag. It was empty.

"Corey?"

She groped for her flashlight and shined it frantically around the tent. She was alone.

Stay calm, she told herself. Maybe he went to the bathroom. That's where he must be. She probably heard him leave without knowing it and that's why she woke up.

Ellen stretched and moved her head from side to side, working the kinks out of her neck. She wasn't used to sleeping on the ground.

She wondered if the zoo security man had gone past yet. She had meant to stay awake and watch for him.

She felt thirsty now so she opened the ice chest and removed a can of juice. After a few sips, she looked outside again.

Corey should be back by now. It didn't take this long to walk to the rest rooms and back.

Ellen put the can of juice down. It would be just like him to decide to go off by himself in search of some excitement. Like it or not, she supposed she had better go look for him.

She walked across the meadow to the rest rooms and cracked open the door to the men's side. "Corey? Are you in there?"

There was no reply. If Corey had been to the bathroom, he was gone now.

She wondered which way he would go and decided it was useless to guess. With her brother, anything was possible. He was probably looking for his dancing zebras and flying giraffes.

At least she didn't have to worry that Corey would get lost. He knew his way around the zoo and no matter which way he went, sooner or later he would come back to the North Meadow. She just hoped he wouldn't try to find the thief and spy on him.

The thief must be a zoo employee—a keeper, perhaps, or a maintenance man. She found it hard to believe that anyone who worked at the zoo would also steal from it but the fence went completely around the outside; no one else could possibly get in.

Or out, she thought glumly.

She decided to take the path to her left first, because she thought that path dead-ended at the north end of the zoo. If Corey had gone that way, she would find him for sure.

She had not gone far when a rustling sound came from the right side of the path. She stopped walking and pointed the light in that direction. Then she smiled. On the other side of the fence sat a whole row of wallaroos, a small kind of kangaroo. They were all up on their hind legs and supported by their tails. They sat still, watching her. Their eyes glowed red as her flashlight reflected off them. Apparently, they were curious about her flashlight and had come to see what it was.

Ellen swung her hands back and forth like the conductor of a symphony orchestra, waving the flashlight in loops and circles. Her parents had taken her and Corey to see a laser light show at the Pacific Science Center once; she wondered if the wallaroos thought this was some kind of laser show.

She continued down the path, pausing now and then to shine her light on each side of the path. When she reached the end, she saw that there was a metal gate blocking this entrance, too. She turned and started back.

The only other animal she saw was a snow leopard, which seemed just as fascinated by her light as the wallaroos had been. After watching Ellen for a moment, the leopard went into its den and then, just as Ellen was going to move on, it came back with a baby leopard.

Clearly, the mother leopard wanted to show her baby the amazing light. Maybe the leopards thought a flying saucer had landed in the zoo and she was an alien being. She realized that was exactly the sort of thing Corey would say, so she beamed the light back at the path and continued on.

Even with the almost-full moon, it was difficult to see where she was. The tall trees with their thick dark branches loomed over her. The flashlight made a small circle of light on the path immediately ahead of her but on both sides and behind her the darkness hung close and heavy. The air seemed thick.

Where was Corey? Where were her parents? She felt isolated from the rest of the world, as alone as if she were walking through the jungles of Africa, where the wild beasts roamed free, instead of here in the zoo where they were contained behind fences.

Although the light helped her see where she was walking, it also made her feel more vulnerable. Anyone or anything in the shadows could see her quickly because of her flashlight, while she could see only what she pointed the flashlight directly at.

She switched off the flashlight and went on without it.

She walked more slowly, putting her feet down carefully, feeling with her toes to be certain she was still on the path.

She heard something move behind her. Holding her breath, she stopped and listened. When she didn't hear it again, she turned on her light and aimed it behind her. She saw only a clump of bushes.

Her mouth felt dry. All around her, the leaves whispered secrets and in the distance, a lone wolf howled at the moon. The mournful sound sent a prickle of fear up the back of Ellen's neck.

She took a deep breath and told herself to relax, but she still had an uneasy feeling, as if some unknown danger lurked just around the corner.

EEIIIYYAHHHH!!!

The scream came with no warning, from the area behind her where she had heard rustling, the place where she had just beamed her light.

Ellen jumped, drawing her breath in sharply. She swung around, instinctively putting one hand across her face for protection. With the other hand she waved the flashlight back and forth, shining it from side to side.

"Who's there?" she croaked. It was a wonder she could speak at all; her throat felt like sandpaper.

There was no answer but she heard that same rustling sound again. It was closer this time. She didn't know whether to turn off the light and run, or try to see who (or what) had screamed.

In the split second that she tried to make up her mind, a peacock stepped into the circle of light. His blue and green feathers fanned high above his tail as he strutted.

"*Eeiiiaayahh!*" he screamed again.

Ellen stared, her heart thudding in her chest. She had always thought that peacocks—or peafowls as she knew they were properly called—were the most beautiful of birds but she had never heard one cry before. It was harsh and shrill, like a cat in pain. How could such a lovely bird make such an ugly sound?

She took a deep breath, turned, and continued down the path away from the peacock. The light jiggled because her hand was shaking. Anyone's hand would shake after that experience, she thought. Any sensible person would fear for her life if a peacock screamed at her in the dark.

She wondered if Corey had heard the peacock's cry. If so, he was probably running for the tent as fast as he could go right now, convinced that some terrible demon was loose in the zoo.

Well, it would serve him right. He knew better than to go off alone this way. When Mom and Dad heard about it, he would catch heck for sure. If Mom and Dad ever heard about it. *Where were they?*

She came to a fork in the path. She stopped, unsure which way to go. Even though she was familiar with the zoo from previous visits, everything seemed different in the dark. She couldn't look off in the distance for landmarks and she was afraid she might have missed some of the signs along the sides of the path.

I should have stayed in the tent, she thought. Eventually, Corey would return. Maybe he already had and, when he found she wasn't there, had gone out looking for her. It could go on that way all night—missing each other, searching in the dark—unless one of them stayed at the camp.

She took the path to her right. If she was guessing correctly, it would wind past the Nocturnal House and back to the North Meadow. She wondered what the Nocturnal House looked like at night. Was it lighted, so the animals would think it was daytime? After she found Corey, maybe she would go to the Nocturnal House and find out. It was close to the North Meadow; she wouldn't get lost. And it would be fun to see her favorite exhibit under different conditions.

The minute she thought of it as her favorite exhibit, she knew where she would find Corey. The monkey house. Of course. It was always his favorite part of the zoo. He had even told Grandma and Grandpa that he wanted to sleep in the monkey house tonight. Why hadn't she thought of that right away?

She walked faster, shining the light back and forth across the path as she went. She hoped she was on the short cut across the middle of the zoo but even if she was on the outside path, she would end up near the monkeys.

And once I find Monkey Corey, she thought, I won't let him out of my sight again.

7

In his mind, Corey was already telling his pals about his zoo night adventure. I went exploring on my own, he would say. I tried to find the thief and spy on him some more. It was pitch black out but I turned off my flashlight and sneaked along, hiding behind bushes, to be sure he didn't see me first.

This time, Corey had his camera. If the man stole something else, Corey planned to shoot a picture and catch him in the act. The police would have proof of a crime.

Corey imagined himself showing the picture to the police and being interviewed by TV and newspaper reporters. He saw himself getting a medal for bravery. Most of all, he thought how exciting it would be to open the newspaper and see his own picture.

The images of glory faded when Corey realized he had been walking a long time and not paying attention to where he was. He should have come to the monkey house by now.

He turned on his light and saw water. A huge hippopotamus lifted his head and opened his mouth. His white teeth shone in the beam of light like a toothpaste ad.

Corey promptly forgot he was The Great Detective. He wondered if the hippo was hungry. Last fall, on the TV news, he had seen the hippos eating whole pumpkins left over from Halloween.

He took an apple out of his pocket. It would be like shooting baskets, only easier, to feed the hippo an apple. Of course, an apple wouldn't seem like much to the hippo. It would be like a person eating one sunflower seed.

Then he remembered that Grandpa had said he shouldn't feed any of the animals because they are on special diets, so he ate the apple himself and walked on. Although he listened carefully and looked in all directions, there was no sign of the thief.

He's probably breaking into the other food stands, Corey thought. Maybe he steals money from them every night. The police and the zoo authorities were certainly going to be glad to learn about this. He and Ellen would be heroes. Maybe they really would get their pictures in the paper. Or maybe just *he* would get his picture in the paper, since he was the one who was going to spy on the man some more and collect additional evidence.

Maybe he should forget about visiting the monkey house. Maybe he should keep hunting for the thief.

No. The zoo covered many acres and the man could be anywhere. He'd look for him again after he found out what monkeys do at night.

It took him longer than he thought it would to find the monkey house. After he left the hippos, he didn't see anything else he recognized. He hadn't thought it was possible for him to get lost in the zoo but he was. He kept on until his flashlight caught a sign with animal pictures on it. One picture was a monkey; an arrow pointed which way to go.

The sign said "Primates." Corey had noticed that the zoo signs and maps always said primates and he didn't understand why. Everyone he knew, even Grandpa and Grandma, called it the monkey house.

He pushed eagerly on the monkey house doors and then sagged against them in disappointment. The doors were locked.

Pressing his face against the glass, he looked inside. Dimly, he saw the benches in the center of the house and the trees in the enclosures nearest the door. He squinted his eyes into narrow slits, trying to spot one of the monkeys.

Something moved in the cage nearest the door. Corey looked that way. It was, he knew, the cage where the tamarin monkeys lived. Grandma and Grandpa had brought him to see the baby monkey after it was born and Corey had entered the zoo's contest to choose a name for the baby. He had suggested Poppy but the zoo committee chose Shadow.

Shadow's mother, Sunshine, was leaping back and forth, running wildly from one side of the cage to the other. Corey stared. He had assumed the monkeys slept at night, but apparently this was their exercise time.

The lights came on inside the monkey house. Corey tried to see who had turned them on but he saw no one. The lights must be on an automatic timer. In the other cages, the monkeys seemed startled by the sudden light. They stretched and looked around.

Sunshine continued her frenzied activity. Several times, she ran to her baby, who was perched partway up one of the trees, and then ran off again.

A banana flew through the air and landed near Sunshine; she did not pick it up.

Was it feeding time now? In the middle of the night? If so, it meant that one of the monkeys' keepers was on duty. That's who turned on the lights. Corey craned his neck, trying to see who had thrown the banana. From his place outside the front doors, he could not see the far corner of the golden tamarins' cage; he could not see who had thrown the banana.

Corey knew Ellen would want him to speak to the keeper. He should explain that he and Ellen were here alone and ask to use a telephone. But if he did, the keeper might make Corey and Ellen go home.

Another banana sailed toward Sunshine. She ignored this one, too. Corey had never seen a monkey act so agitated. Did they always get this excited about being fed?

And then he saw the reason for the mother monkey's distress. Someone had entered the cage from the back side, and was moving slowly, with one hand upraised, toward the tree where the baby monkey sat. The entrance was partway up the back of the cage and the man was on a narrow platform in the tree branches. Corey instantly recognized the tall man in the overalls.

Corey swallowed. It was the same man who broke into

the food stand and took the money. What was he doing now? There wouldn't be any money to steal in a monkey cage.

Corey put his hands on the sides of his face, trying to see the man better. He had wanted to spy on the thief. Well, here was his chance. He would hide here and when the man left the monkey house, Corey would follow him. He would watch to see if the man broke into any other food stands and stole any more money.

Was the man one of the keepers? Was it his job to check on the monkeys at night, to be sure they were OK?

The man crouched and sat motionless on the platform for several seconds. The mother monkey continued to race back and forth. Because of the thick glass partitions, Corey could not hear anything but he was quite sure Sunshine was chattering.

The man reached in his pocket, removed a square package, and tossed it to the ground. A sandwich? Is that what the monkeys eat at night? Corey wondered. Shouldn't the man have unwrapped it? The package had barely hit the ground when the man lunged, reached one arm down into the tree, and plucked the baby monkey from the branch.

The man tried to stuff the baby monkey inside his jacket while the monkey struggled to get away. The mother monkey leaped toward the man; he kicked at her and she retreated.

Holding the little monkey firmly with both hands, the man turned quickly and disappeared through the opening at the back of the cage, closing the door behind him.

The mother monkey went wild. She careened up and down, back and forth, so fast that it looked like she was doing trampoline tricks.

Corey's scalp tingled as he realized what he had witnessed. He felt like a bolt of lightning had just zigzagged from his ears to his toes, leaving all of his nerves crackling with electricity.

He was sure that the tall man was not supposed to take Shadow out of the cage. He was not supposed to feed the monkeys, either. He was not, Corey realized, a zoo employee at all. No zoo employee would act the way this man was acting.

If he doesn't work at the zoo, how did he get in? Who was he? Why would he want to take a monkey? To set it free? Corey had seen a TV special once, about animal rights activists who had freed some caged animals from a traveling circus in order to call attention to their improper care.

But the Woodland Park Zoo was known all over the world for the good way they treated the animals. That's why Grandpa and Grandma always went to the charity auction. They said the zoo had even trained some of the rare tamarin monkeys to survive in the wild and had then set them free in the rain forests in Brazil.

It wouldn't do any good to turn a monkey loose in the city of Seattle. It would never survive.

Maybe he planned to sell it. Some people want exotic pets. Was there a black market for stolen monkeys? Had the man taken animals before? Corey didn't remember hearing about any stolen animals but he wasn't very faithful about keeping up with the news, except for the Sea-hawks and the Mariners.

Corey wished he could get to a telephone, to call 911. That was the emergency number and Corey was sure this would be considered an emergency. He couldn't call 911 when the telephone was on the other side of the fence.

He needed help but try as he might he could not think of how to get it. Even if he ran to the gate and yelled, no one would hear him. The only thing on the other side of the gate was the zoo parking lot and there wouldn't be anyone there at night.

He decided the best thing to do was his original plan: follow the man and watch him closely. He would see exactly what the man did with the monkey; he could report everything to the police tomorrow morning.

Specific, he told himself. Get the specific details.

Corey turned away from the glass doors. He wondered how the man had gotten inside the monkey house. There must be a back door of some sort. Corey had to find it fast and get evidence of what he had just seen. He would take a picture of the man with the baby monkey.

He hurried around the side of the building, toward the back of Shadow's cage. He found the door easily; it was standing wide open and the lights inside were on.

Corey squatted down a few feet to one side of the door. He put down his flashlight and looked through the viewfinder of his camera. If the man left the lights on, Corey might be able to get a picture without using the flash.

"*Chit-chit-chitchitchit.*" The frantic cries of the little

monkey came from inside the door. Corey could hear the mother monkey's screams now, too.

Just as Corey peered through his camera, the lights went off. He lowered the camera. He couldn't use the flash; the man would see it for sure and know that Corey was watching him.

"Damn it!" the man muttered. "Hold still. Stay in there."

The man's back was to him. Corey stayed low. As long as he didn't move, he was sure the man wouldn't see him. There were scuffling noises and the man cursed again.

The man kicked the door, to close it, and started toward Corey. The man's hands were clutched across his chest. Corey couldn't see any monkey but he knew the man was holding one.

The man's arms kept moving, as if he were having trouble holding the monkey. Twice he stopped and struggled with the bulge in his jacket.

A few more feet, Corey thought, and he'll be past me. Then I'll follow him. I'll find out where he takes the monkey. I'll stay behind him and spy on him all night long.

The dark shape of the man loomed over him. Corey held his breath.

And then the man yelped in pain.

Thunk! Fur brushed past Corey's face. Instinctively, he reached out and tried to grab the monkey. The tail slipped through his fingers just as the man dove downward.

The man's hands closed around Corey's arm. He gasped in surprise. Then he grabbed Corey's shoulders and hoisted him to his feet. He muttered something that would get Corey grounded for a month if he ever said it.

Chattering wildly, the baby monkey ran past them and disappeared into the night.

"Who the hell are you?" the man hissed. Before Corey could reply, he added, "You just made me lose $20,000."

Corey had never heard anyone sound so angry. So full of hate.

"I didn't do anything," Corey protested. "The monkey got away all by itself. We have to find it! What if it climbs over the fence?" Corey thought of the heavy traffic on Aurora Avenue or North 50th Street. He shuddered.

"Damn thing bit me." The man shook one hand several times and then put his mouth briefly on his wrist. He spat.

Corey stepped backward but the man quickly gripped him again. His fingers dug into Corey's arms as he leaned closer, staring at Corey. "Maybe," he said slowly, "there's more than one way to collect a ransom."

Corey twisted, trying to wriggle loose. The strap on his camera broke and the camera fell to the ground. "You're hurting me," he said.

"You think that hurts? You don't know what it is to get hurt."

Corey remembered the knife.

He didn't say anything else.

8

ELLEN was lost. She didn't understand how it could have happened, but she didn't know where she was or which way to go to find the monkey house. How could she be so turned around in a place she had visited so many times?

She should have taken a map. Maybe the maps show where telephones are located. But she hadn't known she'd be alone, searching for Corey. And she hadn't known how scarey the zoo would seem at night.

The moon disappeared behind some clouds; it was even darker now than it had been earlier. The path seemed endless and she had no idea whether she was still on the shortcut or whether she had somehow followed another path by mistake. When she waved her light around, nothing looked familiar.

She saw another food stand and moved cautiously toward it. When she was next to it, she stopped and listened in case the thief was inside. She heard nothing.

This, she decided, was the most horrible night of her life. She had looked forward to it so much and now everything had gone wrong. If only she had waited at home until Mom and Dad got there, instead of rushing away in a cab.

"You can't solve a problem by saying, *if only*." That's what Mom always said. Ellen trudged onward.

The beam from her flashlight hit fencing. Ellen stopped and raised the light higher; the fencing continued. She recognized the Aviary. That isn't where she had thought she was, but at least she had her bearings now. The Aviary was close to the monkey house. She had just taken the long way to get there.

Relieved, she walked faster. With any luck, Corey would be in the monkey house. He was probably jumping on one of the benches, scratching his armpits, or hanging by his knees from a railing, pretending to be a monkey in a tree. She would insist that he return to the tent with her and stay there until morning. No more wandering around the zoo in the dark.

Just ahead, she heard a shrill chattering. A monkey?

Yes. There it was again, even louder this time, and she was sure it was a monkey. The monkey didn't sound very happy. It sounded upset, as if someone were teasing it.

The closer she got to the monkey house, the more distressed the monkey sounded. It seemed to be only one monkey and it sounded like it was in pain. Was it hurt? If so, she knew Corey wasn't responsible. Her brother was silly and made up wild stories but he was basically a good kid and he loved the monkeys. He would never hurt one of them.

Light from the monkey house shone out through the glass doors. Ellen saw it and began to run. By the time she got to the monkey house, the chattering had stopped.

The monkey house was locked. Ellen looked through the glass doors. In the first cage, she recognized one of the rare golden lion tamarins that Grandma and Grandpa had brought her to see, when a baby monkey was born. The monkey was clearly upset, rushing frantically back and forth in its cage.

When she looked closer, she could tell it was the mother monkey, Sunshine, the one Ellen had watched as it nursed her baby. What could have happened to distress her so? Was her baby sick? Ellen could not see the baby monkey. It must be in the far corner, she thought, where she couldn't see.

Although she was certain the monkey was making noise, the soundproof glass of the cages and the thick doors of the building prevented her from hearing it. Ellen wondered how she heard the chattering earlier when she couldn't hear it now. Were there monkeys elsewhere in the zoo?

The monkeys in the other cages moved about restlessly while Sunshine leaped hysterically from the tree to the ground and back again.

Ellen heard the chattering again, fainter now. It came from behind the building. From outside. Maybe it was Corey, pretending to be a monkey. She hurried in that direction, flashing her light around. "Corey?" she called. "Are you here?"

"*Chit-chit-chit-chit.*" The excited chattering retreated.

Ellen waved her light back and forth across the back of the building. A door marked "Employees Only" stood slightly ajar. The wood around the lock was splintered; someone had broken in.

Oh, Corey, she thought. Surely you wouldn't have done this. You said you wanted to sleep with the monkeys but you wouldn't do a stupid thing like this. Would you?

Of course not. She answered her own question. Corey was no hoodlum. He didn't go around vandalizing public property and he definitely would not do anything to scare the monkeys. Grandma and Grandpa had taught them that animals have feelings, much like people have. Grandma even carried a list in her purse, of companies that don't test their products on animals. She wouldn't buy soap or shampoo or perfume unless the manufacturer was on her list. Grandma said she didn't want some poor rabbit blinded just so she could smell good.

Ellen continued around the outside of the building, aiming the light toward the ground. Something crunched under her shoe. Looking down, she saw peanuts spilled on the path. Then she noticed red drops on the path near the peanuts. She leaned down to look more closely.

Blood. There were drops of blood on the path behind the monkey house.

Ellen's breath came faster. Had someone hurt the baby monkey? Is that why the mother was so upset?

The man she had seen carried a knife. After he broke into the food stand, he must have broken into the monkey house, too. But why? Who was he? Not an employee of the zoo. She was convinced of that.

But if the man they had seen did not work at the zoo, how did he get in? Where was the security guard? Had they just missed him, or had something happened to him? The questions bounced in her brain like the bumper cars at the county fair.

She stared down at the path. Corey had brought peanuts with him. Were these some of his? How did they get spilled?

Don't jump to conclusions, she told herself. Anyone could have spilled peanuts on the ground. She swung the flashlight in a wider circle, and froze. There, lying on the path a few feet in front of her, was a camera. She picked it up and turned it over. Her hand began to shake.

Mom had taped the small identification tag on the camera before Corey went to camp last July. Corey Streater, it said, and gave the telephone number. Corey treasured his camera. He would never be careless with it.

Ellen aimed the light at the path again and found Corey's flashlight.

Something terrible had happened to her brother. She knew it. He would never leave his flashlight and his camera like this.

Why was blood on the ground? Was it monkey blood—or human?

Where was Corey?

I have to find him, Ellen thought. First, I'll go back to the tent. He's had plenty of time to explore the zoo and if nothing has happened to him he might be back at the tent by now. If he's there, we'll stay inside the tent until morning if I have to sit on him the rest of the night.

If he isn't there . . .

She didn't want to think about what she would do if he wasn't there.

She headed back toward the tent. Please be there, Corey, she thought. Please, please be there.

She never made it back to the tent.

9

As ELLEN passed the Nocturnal House, she heard voices inside.

Her first instinct was to rush in, to see who it was, but she forced herself not to. Instead, she eased cautiously toward the door that leads to the viewing walkway. She pushed it only until she could hear clearly through the crack. It was light inside, to make it seem like daytime for those animals.

"What's a kid like you doing here alone in the middle of the night?" The man's voice was angry. "What'd you do, run away from home?"

"I'm on a camp-out," Corey said.

"Sure, you are. And I'm the Boy Scout leader."

"My grandparents bought the camp-out at a charity auction."

"Your grandparents are here, too?" The man sounded alarmed.

"Yes," Corey said, without hesitation. He was so convincing that for a moment Ellen wondered if Grandpa and Grandma had come to the zoo while she was off looking for Corey. "My sister's here, too," Corey continued, "and both my brothers and my mother and father, and all of my aunts and uncles and cousins. Even some of our neighbors."

"You're lying," the man said. "If all those people were camping out at the zoo, I would have heard them."

"You'll hear them soon," Corey said, "because they'll be looking for me."

There was a brief silence. Then the man muttered, "Well, they won't find you. You and I are going on a little camp-out of our own and we're going to stay there until all those relatives of yours cough up twenty grand."

"You mean you're going to hold me for ransom?" Corey's voice was higher than usual and the question ended with a little squeak.

"Smart kid. Now shut up and let me think."

"But my parents don't have any money," Corey said. "My father is crippled and blind and my mother has AIDS from a blood transfusion that she got. Neither of them can work. There's no way they can pay you a ransom."

Ellen's jaw dropped. She had heard Corey tell some crazy stories before but this one topped them all.

"People who go to charity auctions have money. Now shut up!"

Silence.

Ellen eased the door closed and stood outside in the darkness. Her throat felt tight. She wanted to burst into tears and run back to the tent and hide, but she knew she couldn't do that. Somehow, she had to help Corey. She had to get him away from the man.

I'll climb the fence, she decided. I take gymnastics lessons; I'm strong. I'll go back to the south gate, climb the fence, and call the police.

She hurried along the path, walking as quickly as she could in the dark. When she was past the house where the great apes live, she turned on her flashlight again and began to run. Past the Family Farm, past the open-air theater, past the food stand. By the time she reached the south gate, she was out of breath. She stood for a moment, panting, and looking up. There were brick walls on both sides of the entrance. Wooden lattice, covered with vines, made a canopy overhead for several feet in front of the walls. There was no way she could get through that.

She went toward the exit turnstile until the brick wall ended and a chain link fence began. She would have to climb the chain link fence.

You can do it, she told herself. You MUST do it. It's the only way to save Corey.

She stretched up and grasped the fence above her head. Wedging the toe of her right shoe into the fence, she pulled herself up. She tried to get her left foot positioned, too, but when she put her weight on her right foot, it slipped out of the wire fencing. The holes in the fence were not big enough to allow her to get a solid foothold.

She dropped back to the ground. Quickly, she tried again. This time, she managed to lift herself onto her right foot but was unable to put her left foot in the fence. She clung to the fence, leaning into it, unwilling to jump down and start over but unable to continue. She held on tightly with her right hand, leaned over, and untied her left shoe. She kicked her heel against the fence until the shoe came off and fell to the ground. Now she could curl her toes around the fencing. Through her sock, she could feel the wire and grip it.

She removed her other shoe the same way and then, feeling like one of the monkeys, she began to climb. One hand up, one foot up. Next hand. Next foot. Although she knew she must hurry, she climbed cautiously. Even without her shoes, it was difficult to get a solid grip. Twice, one foot slipped out of the wire but she was able to hold on with the other until she could regain her balance.

Reaching above her head, she felt the top of the fence. She was almost there. Going down wouldn't be so hard. She could let her feet slide down the other side of the fence and just hang on with her hands. All she had to do was make it over the top.

She grasped the top tightly with both hands and pulled herself up. She swung her left leg up and crooked her knee over the top. Her leg hit barbed wire.

She reached out, feeling gingerly with her hand. From the top of the fence, three strands of barbed wire angled out toward the parking lot. The cuff of her jeans was caught on the first strand. She tugged. It held fast.

There was no way she would be able to climb over barbed wire. She tried to kick her left leg free. Her fingers ached, from hanging on to the fence. She kicked again. And again. A piece of barbed wire pierced her sock and cut her ankle.

She gave another furious kick. She heard the sound of her jeans tearing and tried to stop in midkick but it was too late. As the material gave way, she lost her balance and fell.

She clutched frantically at the wire as she fell, trying to grab on and stop herself. Her fingers slid too fast; her hands bumped helplessly down the fence and she thudded to the ground.

As she started to sit up, a sharp pain shot through her left shoulder. She lay back down and waited for the pain to subside.

Tears stung her eyes as she lay huddled at the bottom of the fence. She wasn't going to make it over the top.

Gently, she poked her shoulder and winced at the touch of her fingers. A broken collarbone? Bad bruise? She wasn't sure what was wrong but she knew it hurt. Her scratched ankle hurt, too. She would probably have to get a tetanus shot tomorrow, on top of everything else. Then she felt guilty for feeling sorry for herself when Corey was being held hostage.

She did not try to scale the fence again. It wouldn't do Corey any good if she fell off the fence and killed herself. She would have to get help some other way.

She found her shoes and put them back on. Then, holding her left arm close to her side and trying not to move it, she started back along the path toward the Nocturnal House.

How long had she been gone? Ten minutes? Fifteen? Were the man and Corey still in the Nocturnal House? She didn't turn on her flashlight, for fear the man was nearby and would see her.

As she walked, she tried to think. Where was the security guard? Had something happened to him? Or was he somewhere on the zoo grounds, able to help her and Corey if he knew they needed it? How could she reach him?

There had to be other telephones somewhere. Where? She couldn't stumble around the zoo in the dark all night, hunting for a telephone. Corey needed help fast.

When she got back to the Nocturnal House, she eased open the door again and listened. Silence. Ellen's throat felt tight. They had left. The man had taken Corey somewhere and now she would never find him again.

Just as she let go of the door, she heard a slight sniffling noise. She recognized it immediately as the sound Corey always made when his allergies acted up or when he had been crying. She could almost hear her mother saying, "Corey, stop that sniffling. If your nose is running, get a tissue."

They were still inside. Maybe the man was hiding, unsure how many people were looking for Corey.

She tiptoed a few feet away from the Nocturnal House, where she wouldn't be seen if the man decided to leave. Quickly, she figured out a plan.

She would yell out, as if she were calling to other people, that she had found Corey. She would make it sound like a whole group was on their way to the Nocturnal House.

Had the man believed Corey when he said there were other people on the camp-out? Probably. After all, it was unlikely that Corey would be here alone.

The man probably thought there were others here. If

he did, her plan might work. The man might run away rather than taking a chance that he would be surrounded by a mob of angry relatives. And then she and Corey would run, too, and hide somewhere until morning, or until help arrived.

Even if the man didn't run, the security guard might hear her yell and come. He was probably looking for them anyway. It must be after midnight. If the guard checked the tent and found it empty, he would be alarmed. He would try to find them.

By now, maybe Mom and Dad were home and had called the police or the president of the zoo or someone. Even if Mom and Dad weren't home yet, Grandpa and Grandma would be back by now and would find the note. Help might be on the way already.

Maybe I shouldn't yell quite yet, Ellen thought. Maybe I should wait awhile. Stay right where I am and wait for someone to come. Except the security guard might NOT be looking for them. Mom and Dad might NOT be home. Help might NOT be on the way.

She took a deep breath, planted her feet firmly on the path outside the Nocturnal House and yelled as loudly as she could, "This way, everybody. I think I've found him." She waited a few seconds and when nothing happened, she yelled again. "He's over here. In the Nocturnal House. Come on, everyone! This way!"

The door of the Nocturnal House burst open. With the light behind them, the silhouettes of the tall man and the small boy were plainly visible.

Ellen gasped. The man had one arm firmly around Corey's neck. In his other hand, he held the long sharp knife. "If anybody takes one more step," the man said, "this kid won't live."

What have I done? Ellen thought. She stood still, staring in horror at her brother and the man with the knife.

The man looked around. His eyes stopped briefly on Ellen and then, after waiting for a few more seconds, he looked at her again and said, "Come here."

He knows I was bluffing, Ellen thought. He knows I'm the only one out here. She whirled and started to run.

Behind her, Corey cried out.

Ellen stopped and looked back. The man held the knife in the air now, pointed toward Corey's chest.

She couldn't run away. Slowly, she turned and walked toward the man. "Who are you?" she whispered. "What do you want with us?"

10

INSIDE the Nocturnal House, the man kicked at the wall. "Of all the rotten luck. Just when everything was rolling my way, I get saddled with a couple of brats."

"You don't have to be saddled with us," Corey said. "You could let us go."

"Sure. And have you go screaming to Mama and Papa."

"They aren't . . ." Corey stopped.

The man's eyes narrowed. "They aren't what? They aren't here? That's what you were going to say, isn't it?"

Corey didn't answer.

The man nodded his head slowly, as if the pieces of a puzzle had fallen into place. "You kids are here alone. That's why nobody came when you yelled. And that's why you're going to do exactly as I say. Because there's no one to rescue you."

"There's a security guard," Ellen said. "He's on his way here right now."

"No, he isn't."

"Why are you being so mean?" Corey said. "We didn't do anything bad to you."

"No? Well, the rest of the world did. But not anymore. Old Tony's in charge now and you kids are going to make me a bundle of cash. Twenty grand, to be exact."

"Why do you need money so badly?" Ellen asked. "Don't you have a job?"

"Job?" The man started to laugh. "Don't you have a job?" he repeated, as if it were the funniest joke he'd ever heard.

Ellen and Corey looked at each other. Corey shrugged his shoulders.

"What's so funny about having a job?" Ellen said. "Most people have one."

The man quit laughing. "I'm not most people. I'm Tony Haymes. You won't find me grubbing around for eight hours every day, breaking my back so the boss can get rich. No way. Old Tony's too smart for that.

"If you don't have a job," Corey said, "how do you pay your bills?"

"I've been living rent-free." The man started laughing again. Ellen looked at Corey and rolled her eyes. This guy was some kind of a wacko.

"When you're smart enough," the man said, suddenly serious again, "you don't need a job. You can get plenty of bucks without working."

"You steal money, don't you?" Corey said.

"I take what I deserve."

"It's wrong to steal."

"What are you, my conscience?" The man looked at

them with such loathing that both Corey and Ellen took a step backward.

"If you get caught," Corey pointed out, "you'll go to jail."

"Tell me about it."

The way he said, "Tell me about it," made it clear that he already knew firsthand about going to jail. Ellen shuddered. Who was this Tony? And how were she and Corey going to get away from him?

"Listen hard," Tony said. "This is what we're going to do and I don't want any screwups."

Ellen looked at him. She needn't have worried about remembering specific details, when they watched him rob the snack store. The details of this man's face were etched in her brain. She would never forget this face, this voice. Never.

"We're going to spend the rest of the night in the ticket booth, right next to the gate. No matter what we hear or who we see, we're going to be quiet. You got that?"

Ellen nodded. Beside her, Corey nodded, too.

"Good. Because one peep out of either one of you and the other one will never talk again."

Ellen swallowed. Corey slid his hand into hers and held tight. In his other hand, he still clutched the remains of his bag of peanuts.

"As soon as the zoo opens in the morning," Tony said, "we'll be out of here." He jerked his head toward the door. "Let's go."

He made them walk in front of him. Slowly, they went past the flamingos, and down the path past the great apes.

Ellen knew there was one big flaw in the man's plan.

They couldn't spend the night in a ticket booth because the ticket booths were on the other side of the barrier.

She didn't tell the man that, though. Let him think what he wanted. The longer he kept her and Corey on the zoo grounds, the greater the chance that they would be rescued. This is where Mom and Dad would look for them.

Ellen had put the flashlight in her pocket before the man opened the door. She left it there. The slower they walked, the better the chances that help would come.

Corey tugged on her sleeve. She leaned down but kept walking.

"I'm going to escape," Corey whispered.

"No!" Ellen said. "Don't do something stupid."

"What are you kids whispering about?" Tony demanded. "I told you to be quiet and I meant it."

Just then, Ellen stumbled on an uneven part of the path. If Corey hadn't caught her sleeve, she would have fallen. Instantly, Tony was there, too. He grabbed her arm but Ellen knew he was not trying to help her; he only wanted to make sure she didn't run away.

"No tricks," he hissed.

They kept walking. Ellen was unsure where they were. Gradually, she became aware that Corey was dropping the peanuts out of his bag. One by one, every few feet, he took a peanut and let it slide from his fingers to the ground.

He's leaving a trail, she realized, like Hansel and Gretel. He's making a trail so that if anyone is looking for us, they'll know we came this way. Maybe her brother was smarter than she thought.

She reached up and unclasped one of the barrettes from

83

her hair. Then she lowered her hand and dropped the barrette, flinging it slightly to the side so that it would land on the grass and not make any noise. A few minutes later she did the same with her other barrette.

Without the barrettes, her hair hung in her eyes but she didn't care. It was more important to leave clues than to be beautiful and the barrettes were better clues than the peanuts because they could be identified as Ellen's.

Of course, clues were only helpful if someone was looking for them. As far as she knew, nobody was. Grandma and Grandpa might not have found the note; they might have decided to sleep at their own house since they thought Mom and Dad were here at the zoo. And Mom and Dad—well, who knows what they thought or where they were.

"*Chit-chit-chit.*" The soft sound was behind them. Ellen and Corey stopped. So did the man.

"Who's there?" Tony said.

There was no reply.

Corey nudged Ellen and when she leaned toward him he said, "That's the baby monkey."

"Let's go," the man said.

They walked on. Ellen felt as if all of her senses were working on overload. Her eyes struggled to see in the dark; her ears strained to hear any sound; her taut nerves were poised to react, if necessary.

Ahead in the dark, the lion roared.

Behind them, the man cursed.

He's nervous, too, Ellen thought. He didn't plan on having us show up and he isn't really prepared to take us with him.

Maybe Corey was right. Maybe they should try to escape. If they both ran at the same time, disappeared into the darkness in different directions, he couldn't catch both of them. Maybe he wouldn't even try. Maybe he would let them go.

A small voice in her mind answered, but what if he does catch one of you? What then?

There are two of us, she reasoned, and only one of him. Maybe we could jump on him and overpower him.

He's bigger, the small voice replied. And he has a knife.

Before she could continue the debate with herself, Corey took the decision out of her hands. When the lion roared again a few seconds later, Corey whispered, "The moat." And then, before Ellen had time to react, he raced toward the sound of the lion.

"Hey!" Tony yelled.

Immediately, Ellen took off in the opposite direction. She turned on the flashlight and waved it back and forth, acting as a decoy so Corey could get away. She knew exactly where he planned to go. Because she had come to watch Grandma and Grandpa fish from the lion's moat, she knew precisely how the lion's enclosure was laid out. Corey knew, too. There was a metal fence, to keep the people out, and inside the fence there was tall grass that led to a cliff which dropped downward to the moat. It was a long way down and the water in the moat was deep.

As long as Corey stayed on this side of the moat, he would be safe from the lions but he was counting on the fact that the man wouldn't know that. Only someone who had observed the lion area carefully would realize that a person could go under the fence and still be perfectly safe. Corey was betting that Tony wouldn't look for him on the other side of the lion's fence.

Ellen heard footsteps behind her. The man was after her, not Corey. She would have to turn off her light. If she didn't, he would catch her for sure. She switched off the flashlight and turned to her right. She put her right arm out in front of her as she ran, so she wouldn't bump into anything. Her left shoulder didn't throb anymore but she kept that arm close to her chest anyway.

It was impossible not to make noise as she stumbled through the tall ferns and scrub alder. She pushed on and found herself on one of the paths again.

Her outstretched hand hit something. Quickly, she felt a metal railing with more than one rung. But what was on the other side? She ducked down and crawled between the rungs. She was in tall grass now and she stayed on her hands and knees. After only a few feet, as she put one hand out to move forward, she felt nothing. Air. Empty space. She was at the edge of a drop-off.

She heard a splashing sound from below and realized she must be above the hippo pool. She couldn't think of any other water at this end of the zoo.

She tried to remember how far it was from the top of the overhang, where she apparently was, to the water. About four feet, she thought. Close enough that she could probably slide down without hurting herself.

She wondered how dangerous hippos are. What would they do if a person dropped down into their pool, swam across, and escaped out the other side? Do hippos ever attack humans?

As Ellen crouched on the edge of the overhang, she heard movement behind her. Another peacock? An animal? Or the knife-wielding thief?

The man did not have a flashlight. Thank goodness for that. At least he would have to come within a few feet of her in order to find her.

If it was the man, and he saw her, she decided to take a chance on the hippos.

And then she saw him. He stopped about eight feet to her left, on the other side of the railing. He didn't look toward the pool. He turned his back to the water, leaned his elbows on the guard rail, and stood still. She was certain his eyes were scanning the path and the bushes; he was looking and listening, trying to find her.

Ellen hardly dared to breathe. Light clouds drifted across the moon again. The man was a black silhouette, looming beside her.

———

COREY ran. He didn't hear anyone coming after him; the man must be chasing Ellen. He hoped the man didn't catch her. Maybe it had been wrong to bolt like that. He had been thinking only about how to escape. He didn't think that he might put Ellen in jeopardy.

The lion's area should be just ahead. He knew all about where the lions can and can't go, from when he had come to watch Grandma and Grandpa fish in the moat. His plan was to squeeze under the fence and go to the edge of the cliff, behind the trees. It would be hard for anyone to see him there, even in the daylight. In the dark, it would be impossible.

The man would be afraid to go into a place where wild lions live. He wouldn't know about the steep cliff that went to the edge of the moat or about the hidden fence at the bottom. He wouldn't know that the lions couldn't get to the cliff, even if they swam across the moat.

"*Chit-chit-chit.*" The sound came out of the dark. It was the same sound he had heard a few minutes ago. It still sounded to him like the baby monkey. Maybe Shadow was following him.

Corey stopped running and looked around but it was too dark to see what had made the noise. He wished he hadn't left his flashlight by the monkey house.

He should have reached the lions by now. Had he been mistaken about where he was when he broke away from the man? What if he had run the wrong way? Had he gone in circles, the way people do when they're lost in the woods?

Corey waited, listening.

"*Chit-chit-chit.*" There it was again, just to his right. He thought it was Shadow, but what if he was wrong? Maybe it was Tony, pretending to be a monkey so Corey would come closer.

Where was he? Which way were the lions?

There was a rustling in the bushes. Corey saw only the outlines of trees and shrubbery. He squinted, trying to see if there was a small animal shape, too.

"*Chit-chit-chit.*" The sound came from behind him

now. Corey turned and saw movement at the base of a tree. It was the baby monkey.

Corey dropped to his knees. "Hello," he whispered. "Don't be scared." He held out one hand, in case the monkey wanted to sniff his fingers the way dogs do when they first meet a person.

The monkey didn't move. Corey inched closer. If he could catch the baby monkey, he would do it. The little monkey would be safe with him and Corey could keep it until they were rescued. Ordinarily, he would never try to catch a wild animal but this was an emergency. He could make sure that Shadow didn't escape from the zoo and get hit by a car or some other terrible fate.

"Good little monkey," Corey whispered. "Good Shadow." He moved closer.

"*Chit-chit-chit.*"

Slowly, Corey crept closer to the baby monkey. He wished he could tell the monkey not to be afraid.

He should have paid more attention to Ellen's science fair project. Ellen told him how to talk to Prince, and Corey tried a few times, but he never could concentrate the way he was supposed to. Instead of focusing on Prince, he always made up stories in his mind, imagining what Prince might say to him. Ellen sent the same thought, over and over, but Corey got bored with the same thought and soon gave up trying.

If Ellen were here, she might be able to talk to the monkey, tell it that they were his friends and he would be safe with them. Ellen might be able to coax the monkey to come to him.

But Ellen wasn't here. She was somewhere in the dark

zoo, fleeing from the evil man. What if the man had caught her? He would be angry because they had tried to escape; what would he do to Ellen?

It's my fault, Corey thought miserably. If I hadn't pretended to see Mom and Dad, we would not be alone in the zoo with a madman. What if he caught Ellen and took her out of the zoo and hid her somewhere and tried to collect a ransom and Corey never saw Ellen again? What if . . .

Corey felt something brush his sleeve. Startled out of his horrible fantasy, he looked down and saw the baby monkey standing beside him.

Slowly, Corey put his hand forward and stroked the monkey's head. The monkey didn't move. Corey petted it again. Gently, he put his other hand on the monkey's stomach and picked the monkey up.

He held it against his chest and the monkey snuggled against him.

"It's OK," Corey whispered. "You're safe with me."

As he stood up, the monkey put its arms around Corey's neck. I'll go back to the monkey house, Corey thought. That's probably the last place in the zoo that the man would go now. I'll be safe there and I can put Shadow back in the monkey cage, where he belongs.

I'll find the main path again, and stay on it until I come to the monkey house.

"Don't be scared," he told the monkey. "I'll take you back to your mother."

He was not at all sure of his directions but he started out, carrying the baby monkey. Sooner or later, he would come to something he recognized and then he would know which way to go.

He walked slowly, cuddling the little monkey against him. He wished someone could take a picture of him. He wanted to remember always how it felt to hold the baby monkey. Maybe, when he grew up, he would work in a zoo. He would protect animals like the golden lion tamarin and keep them safe.

There were bushes with thorny spikes around him now; the sharp spines snagged his shirt as he pushed his way through. He tried to think where in the zoo he had seen bushes like these. Was it over by the llamas or in front of the hippo pool? He couldn't be clear over by the llamas; he had not run that far.

He must be near the hippos. Yes, he was near the hippo pool which meant he was close to the main path. Soon he would find it. Soon he could start back to the monkey house.

11

ELLEN'S legs ached. She had crouched there, beside the hippo pool, for several minutes. Why didn't the man leave? He must be waiting for her to move, to make a noise, so that he would know where she was.

Well, Ellen wasn't going to move. Her legs felt like they were rusted shut at the knees and might never straighten out again but she stayed still.

The man cursed. He turned around, hit the railing with his fist, and cursed again. Then, muttering to himself, he walked away from the pool.

Relief flooded through Ellen. He was leaving. She was safe. She could stay right here at the edge of the hippo pool until morning, and he wouldn't find her. He wouldn't find Corey by the lion's moat, either, she was sure of that, and by morning someone would come looking for them.

Her taut muscles relaxed slightly.

She heard the sound of the man moving away from her.

"HA!" he shouted. "I got you, you little bugger!"

Ellen gasped. She scrambled to her feet and whirled in the direction of the man's voice. Her legs, numb from her cramped position, threatened to buckle. She reached for a tree trunk to steady herself.

She heard Corey's scared voice. "Let go of me."

Tears of frustration stung Ellen's eyes. Corey wasn't safe by the lion's moat. He was back in the clutches of the man with the knife. What had gone wrong? Did Corey get mixed up in the dark and run the wrong way?

"*Chit-chit-chit-chit-chit.*"

There it was again. The same sound she had heard earlier.

"Stop it!" Corey cried. "You're scaring him."

Him? Who was with Corey?

"Be quiet and do what I say."

"*Chit-chit-chit-chit.*"

"You made him run away!" Corey said.

"Call your sister," the man commanded.

Ellen didn't move. She held her breath.

"Ellen?" Corey sounded panicky now.

"Call her again. Louder."

"Ellen!" He was crying now; she could tell by the way his voice quavered.

Ellen was quiet. If she let the man know where she was, she and Corey would both be hostages again. That wouldn't help Corey. If the man didn't find her, maybe she could still sneak away and get help.

"She can't hear me," Corey sobbed.

"How do you know? Do you know where she went?"

Ellen heard Corey gulp, the way he always did when he was trying not to cry. "She was going to hide by the lions."

What's he doing? Ellen wondered. Why does he want the man to go back to the lions? Corey must think he can still get away and hide by the moat. Why else would he say that?

Silently, she pleaded with her brother. Don't do anything foolish, Corey. Don't try to escape again. It isn't worth the risk. Just do what the man tells you to do and I'll get help.

Somehow.

Ellen's head throbbed. She wished she could take a couple of aspirin. She knew there were probably some aspirin in the first-aid kit that Mrs. Caruthers had left in the tent but the tent was on the other side of the zoo. It might as well be on Mars, for all the good it did her.

She heard movement. Neither the man nor Corey said anything more but Ellen could hear the sounds as they moved farther away from the hippo pool. If she followed, would the man hear her? She couldn't go the other direction; the hippo pool was there.

She waited until she couldn't hear them anymore. Then, moving as cautiously and quietly as she could, she made her way toward the railing and returned to the path.

She tried to think if there were any parts of the zoo she had not been that night, places where there might be a telephone. Did the security guard have an office somewhere or did he just walk around all night? Where WAS he? If she couldn't get out of the zoo, she had to do something to bring help here. But what?

There were plenty of dry leaves on the ground; she could rub sticks together to get a spark. A fire would bring help.

The animals were fenced in. What if the fire blazed out of control? She couldn't start a fire at the zoo, not even to help Corey.

An airplane buzzed high overhead. Ellen pointed her light straight up in the air and turned it on. Then she put her hand over the end and blocked out the light for a second. She rapidly put her hand on and off the light so that if anyone was looking down from the sky, they would see the light flashing on and off.

Dot, dot, dot; dash, dash, dash; dot, dot, dot. She tried to flash an SOS signal, using the Morse code. She hoped she was remembering the code correctly. She had learned a few signals as a science project last year but she hadn't used the code since she finished the project. Still, the three dots, three dashes, three dots, stuck in her mind and she flashed it several times, until she could no longer hear the airplane.

She knew the chances were slim that anyone in an airplane would see her small light. She had flown once, when her family went to Disney World. She remembered sitting next to Dad, looking out the window of the plane at the tiny houses down below. They had seemed like toys rather than real buildings.

Before they landed in Florida, Dad had pointed out small patches of blue, no bigger than postage stamps, and told her that those were swimming pools. They had laughed together when Dad said he hoped the pool at their motel was bigger than that.

Dad, she thought, *why haven't you come? What happened to you?* She knew something was terribly wrong, or her parents would be here by now. And Grandma and Grandpa, too. If they had got home, they would have checked the telephone machine; they would have seen her note. And they would immediately have arranged to get in the zoo. But none of it had happened. *Why not?*

She tried to think what to do.

I'll have to scream, she decided. I'll go to the gate and I'll scream for help as loudly as I can.

Probably the man with the knife would hear her but maybe someone else would hear her, too. Someone who could help. She knew it was a risk but she decided it was a chance she had to take. She had to do something and, since she couldn't get out of the zoo, yelling seemed to be the best way to bring help in.

With the decision made, she felt better. She paused a moment, trying to think where her chances of being heard would be the greatest. It would have to be where there wasn't a parking lot between the fence and street. Otherwise, no one would hear her, no matter how loudly she yelled.

Maybe, she thought, I should go through the Elephant Forest. She was close to that and she knew the back side of the Elephant Forest adjoined Aurora Avenue North, which was one of the main streets in Seattle. She didn't know exactly how close the street was to the back of the zoo, but she had heard cars going past when they were bathing Hugo.

She wasn't afraid to go into the Elephant Forest. She was fond of the giant beasts.

She moved cautiously, trying not to make any noise.

Although her shoulder didn't hurt much anymore, she was glad there was a way into the Elephant Forest that did not require climbing.

She slid down the gully into the clearing at the edge of the Elephant Forest. Except for getting the seat of her jeans dirty, it was an easy slide. At the bottom, she found wooden poles with cables between them—impossible for an elephant to get past, but no problem for a girl. She slipped between two cables. She didn't see or hear any elephants. She hoped it wouldn't frighten them for her to yell for help from their territory. She hurried across the clearing and entered the brush and trees of the Elephant Forest. Ahead, on the far side, she heard an occasional car.

Yes, this was the right place to call for help. It was as close to people as she could get.

It seemed to take forever to make her way through the undergrowth and, as she made her way around shrubs and trees, she knew it would be easy to go the wrong way. She kept listening for the sound of traffic ahead, and went toward it.

Ellen reached the back fence, and gripped it with both hands. She glanced once behind her, listening carefully, but heard nothing. She had no idea where the man and Corey were now.

"HELP!" Ellen yelled. "I'm trapped in the zoo. Someone help me. Please! HELP!!"

Through the trees, she saw the headlights of a car. She

pointed her flashlight toward the car, and waved it back and forth. "HELP!" she shouted, so loudly that it made her throat hurt. She kept calling, over and over, for what seemed like five or ten minutes. "Help. Help!"

And then she heard something, or someone, moving toward her from behind. Had she frightened an elephant? Was one of the beasts stomping toward the sound of her voice?

"HELP," she yelled again.

"HELP," echoed another voice, directly behind her.

Corey.

"Shut up!" commanded the man.

Before Ellen could run away from the voices, the man's hand grabbed her arm.

He had heard her cries.

He had found her.

12

THE AIRPORT shuttle bus stopped at the Streaters' house. Mr. Streater paid the driver.

"Home never looked better," Mrs. Streater said, as she unlocked the front door. "Hello, Prince. Did you miss us?"

"I am exhausted," Mr. Streater said.

They carried their luggage to their bedroom.

Mrs. Streater peered into Ellen's bedroom and then into Corey's. "All the sleeping bags are gone," she said. She turned on the lights in the room she used as an office. It contained a hide-a-bed, and when they had company it doubled as a guest bedroom. It was where Ellen and Corey's grandparents slept when they stayed overnight.

"Nobody's home," Mrs. Streater said.

"Did you think they would be? I knew your folks would take the kids to the zoo, when we didn't get here on time."

"I knew Father would go on the camp-out but I didn't

think Mother would actually sleep in a tent with a cast on her leg."

"Your mother has always been a good sport. And she does love the zoo."

"She probably couldn't stand to stay behind and miss out on the fun," Mrs. Streater said.

"Maybe it's just as well our plane had engine trouble and we had to land in Portland. This way your parents went on the camp-out, after all."

"They'll have tales to tell in the morning," Mrs. Streater said. "Especially Corey."

"It *is* morning. It's after midnight and I am going straight to bed."

"Don't you want to see if there are any messages?"

Mr. Streater shook his head. "We can't return any calls at this time of night anyway. I'll listen to the messages tomorrow."

Mr. and Mrs. Streater got ready for bed. "I wonder if Ellen and Corey are asleep," Mrs. Streater said.

"I doubt if Corey will close his eyes—or his mouth—all night."

Mrs. Streater turned out the light.

Prince whined and pawed at the side of the bed.

"Go lie down, Prince," Mr. Streater said.

Prince whined and pawed again.

"Do you suppose they were so excited about the camp-out that they forgot to feed Prince and let him out?" Mrs. Streater said.

"Anything is possible."

Mrs. Streater sighed, turned on the light, and got up. "Come on, Prince," she said.

"He probably just wants two dinners," Mr. Streater grumbled.

Mrs. Streater went to the kitchen and turned on the light. She put Prince out the back door. While she waited for him to come back, she noticed the piece of paper on the telephone machine.

"Dear Mom and Dad:

We are waiting for you at the zoo."

Quickly she read the rest of Ellen's note. "Mike!" she called. "Mother and Father didn't take the kids to the zoo. Ellen and Corey went by themselves. They took a cab."

Mr. Streater came to the kitchen and looked at the note. "Your folks must have met them there after they went to the doctor. They would never allow the kids to stay there overnight alone. Neither would the zoological society."

Mrs. Streater dialed her parents' home. "There's no answer," she said.

"Of course not. Your folks are at the zoo, having the time of their lives."

Mrs. Streater let Prince in and fed him.

"Are you coming to bed or not?" Mr. Streater rubbed one bare foot on top of the other.

"I'm going to listen to the messages. Just in case there's something from the kids that we need to know."

Mr. Streater leaned against the refrigerator and yawned.

She pushed the button to play back messages and began to jot down names and telephone numbers. One message was Mrs. Streater herself, saying that she and Mr. Streater were in the Portland airport and didn't know when they would get home. There were several "bleeps" on the machine after that, indicating that someone had called but left no message.

"All those calls were probably us, too," Mr. Streater said.

The next message on the machine was from Mrs. Streater's father. He said, "Hello, it's me. Esther and I are on our way to the hospital."

Mr. Streater snapped to attention. Mrs. Streater reached for him and clutched his pajama sleeve while they listened to the rest of the message.

When they heard, "I'll call you tomorrow, after you get home from the zoo," Mr. Streater said, "I don't like this. I don't like this one bit."

Mrs. Streater turned off the answering machine without listening to the rest of the messages. "Where are the kids?" she said. "Even Corey would know better than to stay at the zoo alone."

"Let's not panic. Maybe someone from the zoological society stayed with them."

"But wouldn't they call and tell us that?"

"Maybe they did. Let's listen to the rest of the messages."

They turned the machine back on and played the rest of the messages. There was nothing from Ellen, Corey, or anyone from the zoological society.

Mr. Streater said, "Let's call Mrs. Caruthers."

Mrs. Streater looked up her number and dialed it. After six rings, a sleepy male voice said, "Hello?"

"I'm sorry to disturb you so late at night," Mrs. Streater

said, "but I need to speak with Mrs. Caruthers. It's urgent."

"She isn't here. This is her son."

"Do you know anything about the children who were going to camp overnight at the zoo? This is their mother and we had plane trouble and didn't get home on time. We have a note saying that the children went to the zoo."

"That's right; the kids are at the zoo."

"Do you know where? If we go there now, do you know where we can find them?"

"You can't get in now. All the gates are locked at night."

"Are you certain that's where the children are?"

"Positive. Ma called a little while ago and she said the kids got there a half an hour late. She was glad she didn't have to wait any longer than that because . . ."

"Do you expect her home soon?" Mrs. Streater didn't mean to be rude and interrupt, but she was anxious about Ellen and Corey.

"She won't be home until morning."

"Oh," Mrs. Streater said. "She stayed, then?"

"She said she couldn't leave, not when . . ."

"How kind of her!"

The voice at the other end stifled a yawn.

"Thank you so much," Mrs. Streater said. "I'm sorry I woke you up. We'll go to the zoo first thing in the morning to bring the kids home."

She hung up, turned to Mr. Streater, and said, "Mrs. Caruthers stayed at the zoo. Wasn't that nice of her?"

"She probably didn't have any choice. Corey probably refused to leave."

"We must do something special, to thank her. Maybe we could send flowers."

"Well, let's wait until daylight to order them," Mr. Streater said, as he returned to the bedroom.

"As long as I'm up, I'm going to call the hospital," Mrs. Streater said. "Maybe someone can tell us how Mother is." Just as she reached for the telephone, it rang.

"This is Jeff Caruthers. You called for my mother a few minutes ago. I was kind of fuzzy minded on the phone but after you hung up, I realized exactly what you had said. Aren't you at the zoo now?"

"No. That's why I called you. Our plane was late and we just got home."

"Ma said the kids came to the zoo alone and met you there a few minutes later. She said she left as soon as you arrived."

"She isn't with them? She didn't stay at the zoo?"

"Ma's at the hospital. My sister's having a baby."

"Then who's with Ellen and Corey?"

"I don't know. Ma thought you were."

Mrs. Streater's hand shook as she hung up the phone and called the police.

"I need help," she said. "I think my children are alone at the Woodland Park Zoo."

13

"**S**TOP yelling," the man said, as his arm tightened on Ellen's shoulder.

She tried not to cry but the pain from his hand on her shoulder was excruciating. Blinking back tears, she glared up into his angry eyes.

"Some people heard me," she lied. "Their car slowed down and I saw them point at me. They've gone for help."

"You're bluffing." The man's other hand gripped the back of Corey's shirt. "Even if you aren't, no one can get in here. I should have got rid of you kids as soon as I found you," he growled. "I should have tied you up, too. Or locked you in the snake house."

Too? thought Ellen. Who else is tied up?

"I had the baby monkey," Corey whimpered. "I was taking it back to its mother but he grabbed me and made me lose it." The man yanked Corey's shirt and Corey gulped, to keep from crying.

"Stand still and be quiet," the man said. "I need to think."

A twig snapped. Ellen jumped. Beside her, she felt the man stiffen. Was the baby monkey following them? She peered into the darkness and she knew the man and Corey were doing the same. A large shape moved toward them from Ellen's right and Ellen realized it was an elephant.

They are such big, strong animals, she thought. If only I had their strength. If only they could help us.

And then she thought, maybe they can. The trainer had told her that elephants have the reasoning ability of a third grader. He said some elephants understood thirty different commands. If the elephants were that smart, maybe she should try to talk to them. Maybe they would get her message.

She tried to block everything else out of her mind, the way she did when she sent her thoughts to Prince. It wasn't easy to do when she was so frightened but her weeks of practice helped.

She concentrated only on the large, dark shape that ambled toward her through the trees. *Friend elephant. Help us. We are your friends and we're in danger. Please help us.*

The elephant stopped. It stood quietly for a moment while Ellen silently repeated her urgent plea. *Friend elephant: help us.* The elephant moved its trunk back and forth, sniffing.

Ellen heard movement from her left now. Another elephant?

The first elephant lifted its trunk and trumpeted. The

loud, sudden noise sent chills down Ellen's arms. Was it answering her? Or did it trumpet because it somehow sensed her fear and Corey's? Maybe it just wanted to warn the other elephants that there were strangers in the Elephant Forest.

Farther back in the forest, a second elephant answered.

"We're going to have an earthquake!" Corey cried. "A BIG earthquake."

"What are you talking about?" the man said.

Ellen wondered the same thing.

"Listen to them," Corey said. "The elephants do that when they're scared. They can sense earthquakes before people can. Before the last big earthquake in San Francisco, all the elephants in the San Francisco Zoo trumpeted, just that way, to warn the other elephants that they were in danger. The keeper at the San Francisco Zoo said they wished they had listened to the elephants and left town before the earthquake hit."

For a moment, Ellen believed him and wondered how he knew what had happened in San Francisco. Then she realized it was another of Corey's tall tales. He was trying to frighten the man. Perhaps if the man got scared enough, he would run away, to try to save himself from disaster.

"Corey's right," Ellen said. "We read about it in *Junior Geographic* magazine. The elephants started trumpeting about ten minutes before the earthquake began."

"One man who was visiting the zoo that day got a broken leg during the earthquake when a tree fell on him," Corey said. His words spilled out like water from a pitcher, flowing faster and faster, the way he always talked when he got into one of his stories. "Afterward, he said if he had known that the elephants were trying to warn him, he would have run far away from the zoo and gone somewhere safe to hide, like a basement. Instead, his leg was crushed under the tree and he was almost trampled when the elephants stampeded."

The first elephant stepped closer. Its trunk reached toward them, as if wanting to touch or smell them. The man leaned backward.

Ellen tuned out Corey's voice. She focused all of her energy on sending her thoughts to the elephant. *Good elephant, help us! We need you. The man is evil. Please help us escape.*

The elephant trumpeted again; other elephants replied. There were more of them now and they all seemed close.

Behind her, on the other side of the fence, Ellen heard another car go past. In front of her, and from both sides, she heard movement. Although Ellen could make out only three distinct shapes, she knew that there were several more elephants nearby.

They trumpeted again. And again. The sound filled the night. It bounced back from the paths, from the trees, from the stars.

If the security guard was anywhere on the zoo grounds, Ellen thought, surely he would come to investigate. He would hear the elephants and come to see what was wrong. Even the cars whizzing past on Aurora Avenue would hear this much noise. Maybe someone would wonder what was wrong and call the police.

Keep calling, good elephants. Bring help.

There was another loud eruption from the elephant

chorus. A tingle of excitement prickled Ellen's skin. She was sure the elephants recognized that she and Corey were in danger and they were responding in the only way they could. Would their cries for help work? Would someone hear them and come?

"An earthquake's coming," Corey repeated. "The elephants know that an earthquake's coming."

"Let's get out of here," the man said.

"You'll get away faster if you go alone," Ellen said.

The man grabbed Corey's arm in one hand and Ellen's arm in the other. He started away from the fence, pulling them with him. "We're staying together," he said, "until I collect my ransom. Now, move it."

The elephants kept calling. It was a steady clamor with first one and then another sounding the alarm.

The man moved around the first elephant, keeping lots of space between it and them. Even in the dim light, Ellen could see that it was watching them. Its huge ears were spread wide and its trunk was raised in the air. Just as they passed it, the elephant let out a mighty blast.

The man began to run. Ellen and Corey stumbled along beside him.

The clouds lifted and the full moon once again shed its eerie light. The second elephant approached from their left and the man swerved away from it. Propelled by the man's hands on their arms, Corey and Ellen crashed through the woods while the elephants continued their uproar.

They zigzagged through the elephant obstacle course, making wide swings around each elephant that they saw. Once, the man didn't see an elephant approaching from the side and it reached out its trunk and touched the back of his neck.

The man cried out and then ran even faster. Ellen held her right arm in front of her face, trying to shield herself from scratchy branches that they passed.

They came to the edge of the forest and started across the clearing toward the gully.

The man stopped. Just ahead, Ellen saw a huge elephant blocking their way. It was Hugo, the enormous elephant that they had helped wash. The trainer had said Hugo was ten feet tall and weighed more than six tons. Looming before them in the dim light, he looked even bigger than that.

Behind Hugo, Ellen saw the gully that led out of the Elephant Forest. They could not get out unless Hugo moved.

The man walked to his right, shoving Ellen and Corey in that direction. Hugo turned that way, too. The man moved the other way. Hugo did the same. His ears fanned out to full size.

"Damn elephant," muttered the man.

Ellen looked up, directly toward the small eyes of the enormous old elephant. *Help us, Hugo*, she pleaded silently. *We're your friends and we need help.*

The elephant swayed slightly from side to side as his upraised trunk fanned the air. His big ears framed his face like giant bookends; his long ivory tusks gleamed in the moonlight.

The man let go of Corey and Ellen. He withdrew the knife from his jacket pocket.

"No," Ellen said. "You can't."

Hugo lifted his trunk higher and gave a tremendous bellow.

"The earthquake is starting!" Corey yelled.

"Oh," the man said. He sounded breathless now, and not as menacing as before. In the pale moonlight, the whites of his eyes were wide with horror. "Oh," he repeated.

"Earthquake! Earthquake!" shouted Corey.

"RUN!" Ellen screamed as she bolted away from the man. "Corey! This way!"

The elephants responded raucously.

There was no way to get around Hugo and up the gully, so Ellen dashed back across the clearing and into the forest, toward the other elephants. Despite the size and the frenzied trumpeting, she did not fear the animals as much as she feared the man. The elephants, she felt sure, were trying to help her.

Ellen knew the man was terrified of the elephants. And he was afraid of an earthquake, too. Ellen didn't think he would chase her now, not back into the Elephant Forest. Instead, he would try to save himself. He would try to get around Hugo, leave the Elephant Forest, and try to find a place where he might be safe in an earthquake.

She hoped Corey was right behind her. The elephants were making so much noise that she couldn't tell if he was running with her or had gone in a different direction. Either way, they would meet at the back of the Elephant Forest. She and Corey could go back to the fence and shine her flashlight at the cars going past until someone noticed and came to their aid.

Corey screamed. The high-pitched shriek pierced the air in a brief interlude between trumpetings.

Ellen looked back over her shoulder.

Corey had not been fast enough.

The man had caught him.

14

TONY had his hand on Corey's arm.

Ellen got a sick feeling in her stomach.

"No!" she cried, as she ran back toward Corey and the man. "Don't hurt him. I'm coming back. We'll go with you. We'll be quiet and do whatever you say." Her cries were smothered by the trumpeting of the elephants; she realized the man could not hear her.

The ground shook. Instantly, the thought flashed through her mind: it really is an earthquake. Corey wasn't making it up, after all.

But then she realized that the earth was shaking because all the elephants were hurrying forward, approaching the clearing. The whole herd was stomping its way toward her. She had always been surprised at how little noise an elephant makes when it moves but now, in their excitement, they crunched shrubbery underfoot and the forest trembled.

Corey screamed again. The man yanked on Corey's arm. Corey wriggled free, stumbled, and fell to the ground.

Ellen rushed toward him. In a brief lull between trumpetings, she called, "I'm coming. We won't try to run again. I promise."

"You kids can't be trusted," the man growled. "If I don't get rid of you now, I'll never make it out of here."

Ellen ran toward the man, wondering frantically if she was strong enough to tackle him. Maybe if she came in low, from behind, the blow would make him fall down. She had to try; she couldn't let him hurt Corey.

Corey kicked at the man, trying to knock the knife out of his hand. The man cursed and lunged at Corey.

I can't get there in time, Ellen thought. Tears rolled down her cheeks and made salty puddles in the corners of her mouth.

Corey kicked again.

The man held the knife high. It stopped above his head for a fraction of a second and then plunged downward.

Ellen screamed.

Just before the blade reached Corey, Hugo turned his head, stretched out his trunk, and pushed the man's arm. The knife whizzed past Corey's ear and clinked against the cable.

"What the . . . ?" Tony jumped and looked over his shoulder. Hugo loomed over him. Hugo's trunk reached out toward Tony again, whipping back and forth like a huge gray snake, barely missing Tony's face. At the edge of the clearing, the other elephants trumpeted.

The knife dropped to the ground.

Tony backed away from Corey, keeping his eyes on Hugo. Hugo stared back, his ears still straight out sideways and his trunk writhing.

Corey crawled through the dirt and grabbed the knife. He jumped up again, reaching for Ellen's hand. Together, they stepped away from Hugo and the man.

Tony spun around and dashed across the meadow.

Hugo lunged after him.

Instead of running into the forest, Tony ran to his right. Almost immediately, he knew he had made a mistake.

There was a fence. A high fence. Unable to climb over it, Tony turned to run the other way but it was too late. Hugo stood directly in front of him now. Tony pressed his back into the fence. Hugo lowered his head, to butt Tony.

The other elephants stamped out of the forest. They moved across the clearing to get closer to Hugo, their trunks thrashing about wildly.

One elephant smashed a small tree flat to the ground with one foot as it crashed forward. When it got to Hugo, it stopped and watched, its trunk uplifted, its huge ears spread wide. A half moon of elephants stood around Hugo, like army tanks ready for battle. One after another, they trumpeted.

"Help!" shouted Tony. "Help! HELP!!"

As soon as Hugo stepped toward the man, Ellen and Corey scrambled and clawed their way up the gully, sending dirt and rocks showering down behind them. When they reached the top, they ran down the path.

"Get rid of the knife," Ellen gasped. "If he gets away from Hugo and catches us, we don't want him to be able to get it again."

They passed the high shed where the giraffes stay at night. The fence in front of it was low and Corey flung the knife over the fence into the tall grass and shrubs that grew in front of the shed.

They pounded down the path. Ellen had a stitch in her side from running but she knew they couldn't stop. As they rounded the curve where the zebras had been earlier, they saw a light.

"Zoo security," called a man's voice. "Who's there?"

They stopped running. At long last, they had found the security guard.

Ellen and Corey both talked at once, trying to explain who they were and what had happened.

"I just came on duty," the man said. "Where is the other guard? Have you seen him?"

"No."

"What about the night veterinarian or the keeper?"

"We haven't seen anybody except the man with the knife," Ellen said, "and Hugo has him."

"Hugo who?"

"Hugo the elephant."

"What do you mean, Hugo has him?"

"He has the man trapped against the fence," Corey said, "and he's going to butt him with his head."

"Oh, no!" the guard said. "He'll crush him!"

"He's doing it to help us," Ellen said. "He saved our lives."

The security guard wasn't listening. "You kids stay

here," he commanded. "I called the elephants' trainer when I heard the elephants making such a ruckus. He's on his way. Stay right where you are and I'll try to calm Hugo until the trainer gets here. I don't know where everybody else is but if anyone comes by, send them to the Elephant Forest."

Ellen was only too glad to quit running. She sank down on the path and Corey sat beside her.

"If Hugo kills the man," Corey said, "will they punish him? Will they think he went crazy and that now he's too dangerous to live in the zoo anymore?"

"Oh, I hope not," Ellen replied. Had it been a horrible mistake to ask the elephants for help? If Hugo hurt the man, it was her fault. If they lock Hugo up, Ellen thought, I'll never forgive myself.

"Look!" Corey said.

Ellen looked where Corey pointed. Through the trees, she saw blue lights flashing around and around.

"Police!" Corey cried.

They scrambled to their feet and dashed toward the lights. "Help!" Ellen shouted. "We're in here. Help!"

She saw more lights now and heard voices. "We're here," she cried again. Searchlights suddenly flooded the whole area with brightness. Ellen and Corey stopped running and blinked their eyes, trying to adjust to the harsh, unexpected light.

"There they are," someone yelled.

Moments later, Ellen saw her parents. Her parents and what looked like an entire squad of police officers. Her mother was crying. Her father kept saying, "Oh, thank goodness," over and over.

Mr. and Mrs. Streater ran forward. Mrs. Streater hugged Corey while Mr. Streater hugged Ellen and then all four of them hugged each other at the same time.

A red minivan screeched to a halt just outside the gate and a man jumped out. "I'm the elephant trainer," he said to the police. "I had a call from zoo security that the elephants were restless. What's going on?"

"There's a man in the Elephant Forest," Ellen said. "He had a knife and he tried to kidnap us but all the elephants trumpeted and then Hugo went after him."

"Hugo is going to kill the man," Corey said.

The trainer sprinted down the path toward the elephants. All but one of the police officers raced away, too.

"Who is the man?" the police officer asked Ellen and Corey. "Did he tell you his name? Do you know why he was here?"

"His name is Tony something," Ellen said.

"He stole money from the zoo and he was going to hold us for ransom," Corey said. "He was going to lock us in a room and not feed us and then make you pay billions and billions of dollars to get us back."

"It would have been worth it," Mr. Streater said, as he hugged Corey one more time.

The director of the zoo arrived, and wanted to know what was happening. He said Jeff Caruthers had called him. After the police officer explained, the director said, "It couldn't be Hugo. He's our most gentle, well-trained elephant. He would never be aggressive toward a human."

"It was Hugo," Ellen insisted. "But he didn't attack

the man. He only defended us. He saved Corey's life. And probably mine, too."

The director headed for the Elephant Forest.

"They may need my help," the officer who had stayed with the Streaters said. "I'll be back as soon as I can." He rushed away.

Corey said, "I want to go, too."

"We're staying as far away from that horrible man as we can," Mrs. Streater said.

"The police have guns," Corey said. "What if they shoot Hugo?"

Mr. Streater frowned. "I don't think they would destroy an animal whose home has been invaded. The trainer would use a tranquilizer gun, to make Hugo fall asleep."

"He didn't have time to get a tranquilizer gun," Ellen said, choking on a sob as she spoke. She knew she sounded hysterical but she was unable to control her voice. "Hugo attacked the man in order to save us. If Hugo sees us now and knows that we're safe, maybe he would leave the man alone."

Mr. and Mrs. Streater looked at each other.

"Please?" Ellen said. "He saved our lives. If there's any chance that we can help him, we should do it."

"Let's go," said Mr. Streater.

"Hurry!" said Mrs. Streater.

They rushed down the path toward the Elephant Forest. Thanks to the floodlights that the police had brought, they could see where they were going. Ahead, the elephants trumpeted again.

When they reached the gully, they stopped and looked down. A semicircle of police officers surrounded Hugo. The other elephants had retreated to the edge of the clearing and stood watching.

Hugo still had the man pinned against the fence. Hugo wasn't actually touching him but he kept flicking his trunk from one side of the man to the other. Whenever Tony tried to move, Hugo put his head down, as if he were going to butt Tony with it.

The zoo director stood beside Hugo. The trainer stood against the fence, to Tony's left, where Hugo could see him. The trainer was talking to Hugo, giving him gentle commands.

A crackling sound came from a walkie-talkie that was attached to the belt of one of the officers. The trainer put his finger to his mouth, signaling to be quiet. Ellen saw the officer push a button, to turn the walkie-talkie off.

"Back, Hugo," the trainer said. He held his hand up, with the palm toward Hugo, and pushed it slowly through the air. "Back," he said again.

Hugo lifted one front leg.

"Back, Hugo." The trainer repeated the gesture.

Corey nudged Ellen in the ribs and pointed. She looked where he was pointing and saw two police officers with their guns drawn. She bit her lip to keep from crying out to them not to shoot Hugo.

15

THE TRAINER continued to give clear, short commands. Hugo folded his ears back against the sides of his head, instead of sticking them out sideways. Ellen thought that was a good sign.

The other elephants lowered their trunks. None of them moved or trumpeted.

No one spoke. All Ellen could hear was the faint, low voice of the trainer.

"Back, Hugo." Each time he gave the command, the trainer gestured again.

The big elephant turned his head slowly from side to side. His trunk sniffed the air.

When he looked in her direction, Ellen waved at him. Maybe he would recognize her and know she was safe.

Corey waved, too.

"Back, Hugo. Back."

Hugo stepped backward, away from the fence.

"Good boy," said the trainer. "Back. Back."

Hugo moved backward again.

The trainer stepped away from the fence, toward Hugo. He motioned to Tony to go behind him.

Tony staggered away from the fence, into the waiting arms of a police officer.

Ellen began to tremble. It was as if all of the fear that had consumed her for the past two hours needed to shake itself out of her body. Her legs quivered so badly that she wasn't sure she could stand up. She felt her mother's arms go around her and guide her to a bench. Gratefully, Ellen sat down.

"It's Tony Haymes," said one of the officers whose gun had been ready. "The con who escaped from the state penitentiary yesterday."

Mrs. Streater plopped down on the bench beside Ellen. "Oh, my," she whispered.

"We thought you were going to shoot Hugo," Corey said.

"I'm glad we didn't have to," said the officer.

"So am I," said Ellen. "I think the man was more dangerous than the elephant."

The police officer who had originally stayed with them came over to the bench.

"I'd like to ask you some questions now," he said.

"Corey," Mr. Streater warned, "you must tell the exact truth and nothing more."

Corey got a hurt look on his face. "I wouldn't lie," he said indignantly.

While they were explaining everything that had happened, the other police officers walked out of the elephant area and started down the path. Tony Haymes, with his hands behind him in handcuffs, walked with them.

Ellen watched him go.

The police officer said, "He was in for armed robbery before. When another sentence is added to the first one, he'll probably be locked up for the rest of his life."

What a waste, Ellen thought. The man didn't look more than twenty-two or twenty-three years old. If he had worn clothes that fit properly, he might even have been good looking. Now he would spend his entire adult life in prison.

He thought he was so smart, not getting a job like other people. Well, he didn't look smart now. He looked scared.

He glanced once at Ellen. The anger and hatred that had flashed from his eyes earlier were intensified now, as if he thought it was her fault that he was going back to prison.

Ellen knew better. No matter how much Tony blamed the rest of the world for his problems, he was responsible for what he did. No one else was.

As Ellen watched him pass, the edges of her fear melted a little, replaced by pity. Tony Haymes would not marry or have children. He would never go to a football game or walk on a beach or go fishing. He would never take a vacation and he would never again visit a zoo. She wondered how the chance for some fast money could possibly be worth all those years behind bars.

Corey watched the man walk past, too. "He tried to steal the baby monkey," Corey said.

"The golden lion tamarin?" asked the zoo director.

"Is that a rare one?" asked the police officer.

"Yes," said the director.

"But it got away," Corey said. "Shadow is loose somewhere in the zoo."

"Unless he climbed over the fence," said Ellen.

The director asked them exactly what had happened with the monkey and where it was last seen. Then he hurried off, giving orders to the security guard.

The police officer talked to them for a long time. Finally he said, "We may want to question you again later, but for now you can go home."

"We aren't going home," Corey said. "We're camping overnight at the zoo."

"You can't be serious!" Mrs. Streater said. "Do you really want to stay here after all that's happened?"

"Under the circumstances," said Mr. Streater, "I think we'll cut the camp-out short and go home now."

"But we can't!" Corey cried.

Ellen knew he was worried about his ten-dollar bet but she didn't say anything.

"There isn't any danger now that the police have caught the bad man," Corey said. "And you're here, to stay with us."

Mr. and Mrs. Streater looked at each other. "It's three o'clock in the morning," Mrs. Streater said.

"So the night is shot anyway," Corey said. "We might just as well stay."

Mr. Streater laughed.

The zoo director returned. "We found the guard who was on duty until one A.M.," he said. "He was in the

Animal Health Care office, tied up and gagged. He tangled with Tony Haymes early in the evening."

"Is he all right?" asked Mrs. Streater.

"Only his pride is injured. He said that one of the llamas got kicked by another llama and had a badly shattered leg. The night keeper and the vet took her to Pullman, to the Washington State University veterinary hospital. The guard was placing a call for replacement help for tonight when Tony Haymes jumped him."

"Even after all that has happened," Mr. Streater told the director, "my son wants to spend the rest of the night here at the zoo."

"It's all right with me, providing you stay in the North Meadow," the director said. "All the animals are restless because they heard the elephants trumpeting. And we'll be searching this area for the baby tamarin. I don't want the animals made even more nervous over unnecessary flashlights or noise."

"I'm too tired to do anything but sleep," Ellen said.

"Please, Dad?" Corey said. "It means a lot to me."

Yes, thought Ellen. Ten dollars.

"Ellen?" Mrs. Streater said. "What about your sore shoulder? Do you want to go home?"

Ellen looked at Corey's anxious face. "Oh, my shoulder's OK," she said.

"If we don't sleep here tonight," Corey said, "we'll never get to do it."

"I suppose since we're here, we might as well stay," Mr. Streater said.

"This family," said Mrs. Streater, "will be the death of me."

Corey smiled. Whenever his mother said that her family would be the death of her, he knew it meant she was going to go along with whatever it was that the rest of them wanted to do.

"I do want to call the hospital, though," Mrs. Streater added, "and find out exactly what's happened about Mother's leg."

"There's a telephone just ahead," said the director. "It's outside the rest rooms, near the great apes and the Family Farm."

Ellen groaned. How had she missed it? She must have passed within a few yards of the telephone, but in the dark she had not seen it.

Mrs. Streater was on the phone for several minutes. When she hung up, she said, "Grandma's leg was re-set and she's sleeping now. She'll be home in a few days."

They started toward the North Meadow. Even though the searchlights had been turned off, the zoo didn't seem as dark as before. The trees were less menacing and the night sounds were friendly. Ellen's head even stopped aching.

Several times, Corey scampered ahead and returned, like a puppy whose owner doesn't go fast enough on a walk. Once he said, "Be quiet when you go around the curve. This is where the zebras do the hula."

"What next?" said Mr. Streater, but Corey had already left again.

"We'll have to sleep in our clothes," Mrs. Streater said, when they reached the tent. "We didn't bring pajamas."

"Have a sandwich," said Corey.

126

Ellen thought that was the best suggestion Corey had made all night.

While they ate the rest of the picnic food, each one told in detail exactly what had happened that night—all except the fact that Corey had deliberately misled Mrs. Caruthers. When Mr. and Mrs. Streater assumed that Corey thought he saw them, Ellen didn't tattle on him. She had a feeling Corey already regretted what he had done.

Mr. and Mrs. Streater explained how they waited five hours in Portland. "We called several times and always got the machine. We thought Grandpa and Grandma had come to the zoo with you."

When she heard how her parents had gone to bed but Prince whined until they got up again, Ellen said, "Prince is a hero. If he hadn't scratched and whined, you wouldn't have found our note until morning." Secretly, she wondered if Prince might have received her thoughts long distance, when she asked the elephants to help. Had he known she and Corey were in danger? Was he trying to help them, too?

Ellen put disinfectant on the scratch on her ankle and then, at last, everyone settled into their sleeping bags.

Ellen lay for a long while, unable to fall asleep despite her weariness. She was finally drifting off when she heard, "*Chit-chit-chit.*"

Ellen's eyelids sprang open. Had she dreamed it or had she heard a soft animal sound just outside the tent?

She listened. She heard her mother's even breathing; her dad gave a soft snore. Then it came again. "*Chit-chit-chit.*"

"Ellen? Mom? Dad?" Corey's whisper came from the darkness.

"Mom and Dad are asleep," Ellen said. "Did you hear that noise?"

"It's Shadow," Corey said. "I'm going to catch him."

Ellen unzipped her sleeping bag and sat up. She saw Corey lift the flap of the tent and step out. Quickly, she followed him.

"*Chit-chit-chit.*" The sound was louder now. It came from a small clump of bushes directly behind the tent.

Corey sat on the ground near the bushes. Ellen sat behind him. Neither of them spoke. A tiny face peeked out from behind the bushes. Then the little monkey ran to Corey and, without hesitating, climbed into Corey's lap.

Corey put his arms around the baby monkey. "This time," he said, "I really *will* take you back to your mother."

"This time," said Ellen, "you are not wandering about the zoo alone. I'm waking up Mom and Dad."

Mr. Streater found the zoo security man. He said the director and some other zoo employees were still searching the area near the hippo pool, where the baby monkey had escaped from Corey. Soon the baby was reunited with its mother.

By the time Ellen crawled back into her sleeping bag, she could see the first faint tinge of pink light in the morning sky. She fell asleep instantly and slept soundly until voices outside the tent woke her. She saw that her parents were already up.

Mr. Streater poked his head in the tent and said, "Wake up, kids."

Corey moaned and rubbed his eyes. "I want to sleep some more," he mumbled.

"There's someone here from the newspaper," Mr. Streater said. "He wants to take your picture with Hugo and with the baby monkey."

Corey bounded up, all trace of sleepiness gone.

Ellen followed him out of the tent.

A man with a camera bag stood with Mr. and Mrs. Streater. He held a notebook and pencil. The zoo director was there, too, and the reporter was writing down what the director said.

"Hugo is normally a gentle animal," the director said, "but when he sensed danger, he responded. He could easily have crushed Tony Haymes against the fence. He didn't do it, even though the other elephants were trumpeting and running."

"What made them start?"

"They trumpeted," the zoo director said, "because they heard the children call for help. Then, when three people ran through the Elephant Forest, the elephants got more excited and followed them."

Ellen wondered why the reporter didn't ask her and Corey the questions. After all, they were the ones who were there when everything happened.

"I asked the elephants to help us," Ellen said. "Hugo held Tony against the fence because I told Hugo we were in danger."

The reporter looked startled.

"Ellen," said Mrs. Streater, "I don't think . . ."

"She learned how to talk to animals, for a science project," Corey explained.

The reporter smiled at Ellen and Corey but didn't write anything in his notebook.

The zoo director said, "There were strangers in the elephant enclosure, yelling and disturbing them. Naturally, the elephants reacted by trumpeting and attempting to defend themselves."

Ellen could tell that, except for Corey, no one believed that Hugo and the other elephants had received and understood her messages.

Had the elephants heard her silent cries for help? Did Hugo know what she said?

The zoo director's explanation was logical, she had to admit that. Still, she couldn't help feeling that, last night, the elephants had known what she was trying to tell them.

There was no way to prove it, of course. She wouldn't even include Hugo in her science fair project, since there was no way to document more experiments. But she believed, and would always believe, that he had understood.

"Are we going to have our picture in the paper?" Corey asked.

"Indeed, you are," said the reporter. "First, I want to shoot one of you in front of the tamarin monkey cage and then we'll take one with Hugo."

"Maybe we could be IN the monkey cage," Corey suggested, "looking out through the wire. And what if we sat on Hugo's back?"

"Corey . . ." Mr. Streater said.

Ellen combed her hair with her fingers and tried to

make it stay back out of her eyes. She wished she hadn't thrown away her barrettes last night. Nobody had followed her trail anyway and now she looked like a kitchen mop, just when she was getting her picture taken for the newspaper.

The trainer was at the Elephant Forest, to help Hugo pose.

Ellen's heart filled with love and gratitude when she saw the great gray beast. As she entered the elephant area, she looked up at Hugo and saw that he was gazing down at her.

She stared into his eyes. *Thank you, Hugo,* she thought. *Thank you, dear elephant friend, for helping us.*

Corey nudged Ellen with his elbow. "Listen," he whispered. "Do you hear that?"

Ellen nodded. She smiled up at Hugo. *Thank you,* she repeated. *You saved our lives. We love you.*

"He's purring!" Corey said breathlessly. "I can hear him."

That night, the picture was on the front page. It showed Ellen and Corey standing in front of Hugo. Hugo's trunk rested lightly on Ellen's shoulder.

The headline said, TERROR AT THE ZOO.

Ellen read the article and started to laugh. "Listen to this," she told Corey, and then read one paragraph out loud: "The representative of the Woodland Park Zoological Society who arranged the camp-out was not present. She was at Swedish Hospital, where, at four A.M., her daughter gave birth to twins."

"See?" Corey said. "Nobody ever believes me."